I0760392

ADOPTED

THE ADOPTED SERIES
BOOK ONE

MEGGAN LARSON

For permissions contact:

hello@starfishstoriespublishing.com

E-Book ISBN: 978-1-7774164-4-7

Print ISBN: 978-1-990419-24-9

Hardcover ISBN: 978-1-990419-25-6

Dust Jacket ISBN: 978-1-990419-67-6

1st Edition

Based on a true story (loosely).

Edited by C.B. Moore

Cover Designed by Meraki Cover Design

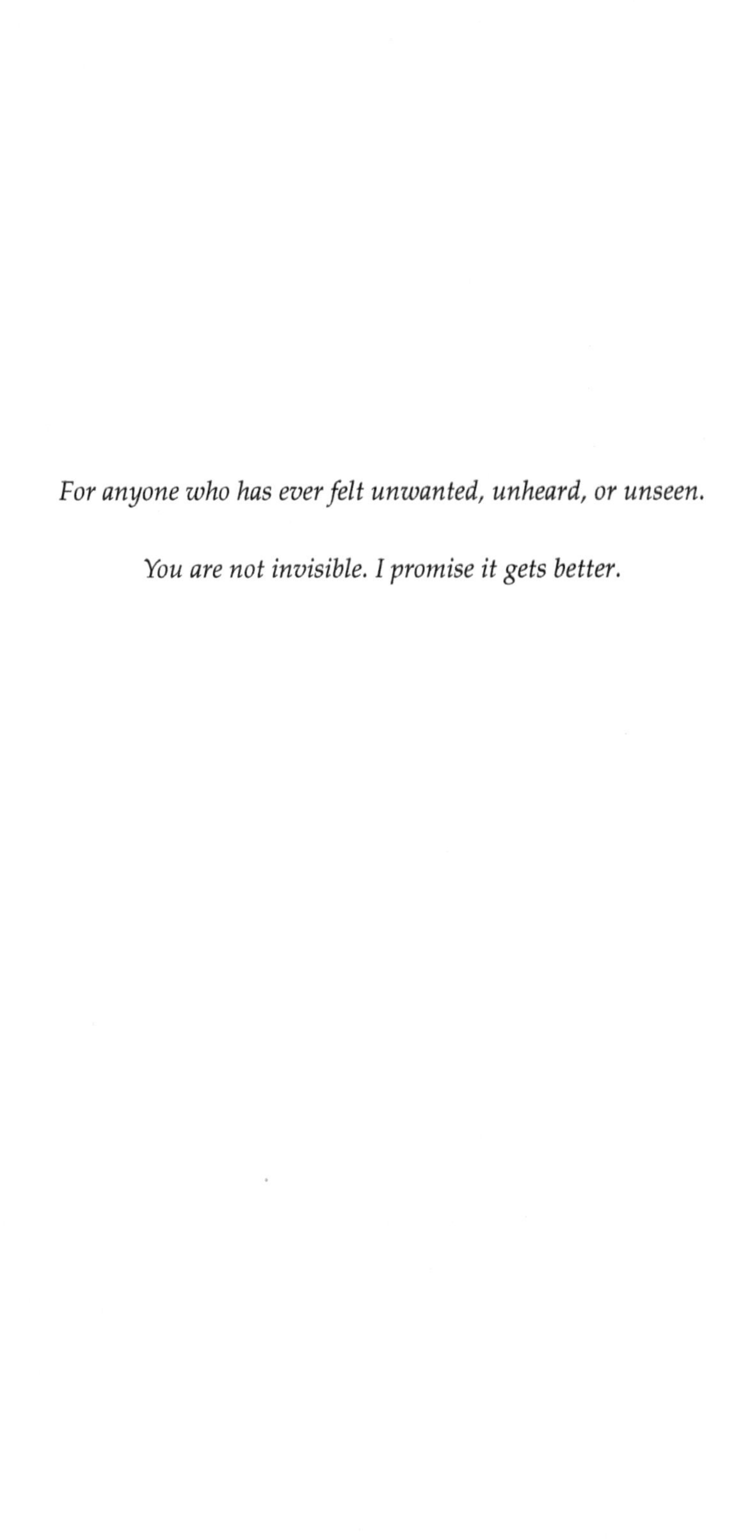

For anyone who has ever felt unwanted, unheard, or unseen.

You are not invisible. I promise it gets better.

TRIGGER WARNING

There is a scene in this book that depicts an attempted sexual assault that may be uncomfortable for some readers.

PROLOGUE

Right on schedule, Ali went into labor two days after Christmas. She glared at Jason and dug her nails into his arm with every contraction, feeling a twinge of satisfaction each time he winced.

"You've been at this for hours, hon. Are you sure you don't want any pain relief?" Ali looked up at the stranger with kind blue eyes asking her the question. She opened her mouth to refuse again but then shrank back in defeat and nodded weakly. She was exhausted. The woman patted Ali's head gently and walked over to the hospital phone.

Ali braced herself for another contraction. They were coming more frequently now, and she squeezed her eyes shut trying to imagine that she wasn't half-naked in a room full of strangers. She wished her mom were here instead of Jason. The searing pain in her abdomen intensified, causing her to scream out loud. More cold hands lifted her gown and touched her in places they had no business touching.

"She's crowning," a man said.

Suddenly the kind-eyed stranger was back, clutching Ali's outstretched hand and speaking softly from behind her mask.

"I'm so sorry, sweetie, but it's too late for an epidural. Your baby's almost here so I'm going to need you to push, okay?"

Ali tried to concentrate on the nurse's words, but it felt like fire was shooting out of her, and all she could do was whimper. She caught a glimpse of Jason backing away to lean on the wall as more medical staff rushed over. Everything was wrong. She shouldn't be here like this. She was too young, her mom wasn't here, and she was terrified. She'd been in a stiff hospital bed all day, being fed ice chips and nothing more just in case a C-section was needed.

The pain wasn't letting up anymore. She screamed and writhed while strangers held her down.

"Push, Ali!" the nurse firmly ordered.

"I can't!" Ali screamed through her sobs. She had never felt pain like this.

"You have to, sweetie. If you don't, then your baby will be in distress and you'll need surgery."

Ali looked into her eyes to gauge whether the nurse was bluffing; she wasn't. Gritting her teeth, Ali found the determination she needed to push. She took a deep breath, clutched the nurse's hand tightly, and pushed with all her might.

"That's it, Ali! Another deep breath…and push!"

Every push felt like it was ripping her in half, but she kept going.

"Here it comes!" the same man cried out.

It was almost over. She pushed one last time, giving it everything she had, then sank back on the bed in relief. All she could hear was the ringing in her ears and all she could see was the blinding lights above her, piercing her eyes like needles. She knew she could sleep for a thousand years and it still wouldn't be enough.

A crying baby broke the silence, and for a moment the sound was so foreign that she almost forgot what had just happened. But then the sound penetrated her heart as though she had never heard anything at all up until that moment. That was *her* baby. She sat up slowly, cautiously, trying to sneak a peek.

"Congratulations, you have a beautiful healthy baby girl." The kind stranger was walking toward her, cradling her baby. Ali leaned forward in anticipation and let the nurse gently place the baby in her waiting arms. Jason reappeared over her shoulder.

"Wow." They whispered it in unison.

Ali wasn't prepared for how beautiful her baby would be. With a head full of dark, curly hair, and the softest skin Ali had ever felt, she was something to fall in love with.

The doctor gestured for Jason to come over. "Do you want to cut the umbilical cord?"

Ali managed a weak smile at the look of terror on his face.

"Isn't there someone more qualified to do that?" Jason asked with raised eyebrows. The doctor laughed and walked him through it.

A couple of hours later, after she had cleaned herself up and the hospital staff had given her fresh sheets and something to eat, Ali lay in bed holding her baby girl. Jason had given her some space but came back almost as soon as she lay back down.

"May I?" Jason asked Ali as he approached her and reached for the baby. She reluctantly gave her up to him and watched as he stared at her lovingly, with tears in his eyes.

"What should we call her?" His voice was barely above a whisper.

Ali looked thoughtfully at him and whispered back. "How about Rose?" Jason smiled and nodded his head as Rose cooed in his arms and fell asleep.

"I'll visit you every day, Rose," he murmured to her.

Maybe this could work, Ali thought to herself. *Maybe we really could do this*. Sure, she was only sixteen—but this was *her* baby. Shouldn't she be the one to raise her? A knock at the door brought her back to reality and her eyes widened as she watched her mother timidly walk in.

"Hi, Ali," her mom said quietly as she slowly walked toward her.

"Mom?" Ali mumbled in confusion. What was she *doing* here? They hadn't spoken in months. She looked beyond her toward the door, and disappointment filled her as she realized that her dad hadn't come.

Ali's mother came over and sat across from her in the stiff hospital chair; then, almost instinctively, she rose and moved to sit on the edge of the bed beside Ali's legs. She leaned forward and brushed Ali's hair back, touching her daughter's forehead with the back of her hand as though checking for a temperature.

"How are you feeling?" she asked.

"I wasn't sick, Mom," Ali muttered.

"I know that, Ali." Her voice sounded a little clipped and she sighed heavily, gently squeezing Ali's leg like she used to, whenever her daughter wasn't feeling well.

Ali studied her mother for a minute. She was well put together, as always, in gray slacks and a yellow cardigan. Her blonde hair was coiffed expertly, but all the makeup in the world couldn't hide the bags under her green eyes or the new worry lines on her forehead.

"Would you like to hold your granddaughter?" Jason asked softly, standing near her mother.

"Um, no. I think that would only make it harder." Ali's mom cleared her throat and looked down. "Could we have a moment?" She motioned for Jason to give them space, and as he backed away his eyes met Ali's, silently pleading with her.

"Ali, don't ruin your life over this." Her mom spoke quietly as soon as Jason stood at the other end of the room. "You're sixteen, with your whole world ahead of you. This…situation has already ruined lives, ours and the baby's included."

Ali's mouth felt bone dry, and she couldn't bring herself to respond. The pattern on the chair beside her was hideous; swirls of brown and black as if the hospital knew it would get stained anyway, so they'd just picked the messiest pattern they could find. As mesmerizing as it was, it couldn't distract her for long. There were too many decisions to be made, and of course, this was the plan. She could *not* take care of a baby. She glanced longingly at Rose in Jason's arms, in the light of the window, and her determination wavered. But maybe she could. Other people did it at her age, didn't they?

"We're almost done raising you and your brother, Ali," her mother continued. "We can't take on a baby. You don't understand how hard it is to raise a child alone."

"She wouldn't be alone," Jason interjected. Ali's mother turned to look at him.

"Didn't I hear that you got fired from two whole jobs in the last few months? How are you going to keep up on all of the bills for three people?" Looking back at Ali, her mother went on. "Why would you refuse to give this baby a better life than you could ever provide? Didn't you already choose a new family for her? How are they going to feel if you go back on your promise? Sign the papers, Ali. Do the right thing." Her mother's words started to echo almost immediately in her head as she squeezed Ali's leg once more, stood, and quietly left the room.

"Ali, come on..." Jason's voice broke the silence as he gently placed Rose back into her arms. Ali watched the nurse come in and fidget with something in the corner, and suspected she was trying to give them some privacy.

"Just give me a minute to think, Jase!"

She hadn't meant to snap at him, but she felt pulled in so many directions. Her mother was right, but that didn't make her want to keep her baby any less. Realistically, though, how was she going to take care of a baby alone? Jason had taken off on her before, who was to say that wouldn't happen again when things got hard? Then what would she do? Fear bubbled up inside her chest.

"She's right, Jase. How *are* we going to pay for stuff? Do you know how expensive diapers are? Your last job couldn't have even covered a week's worth, and you got fired." Maybe he had a plan. Maybe he was about to explain everything and fill her with confidence that this was going to work.

"That's not fair, Ali! You know how they treated me! I couldn't have stayed there anyway." He moaned.

The flowers on the night table—he'd brought them. Carnations, most people's least favorite flowers but the variety most commonly found at gas stations. They'd do for births or deaths. The sun shone through the room and lit them up, showing that some were already wilting; several petals had dropped onto the table. She stared at those fading flowers and imagined the life she'd have with Jason. Those carnations had probably taken an effort for him, and they weren't even good enough for this baby. He might try, but she worried that he would always have one foot out the door. She might always struggle to make ends meet, living on food stamps and government assistance...

"Ali, look at me," he pleaded.

She couldn't bring herself to meet his eyes, so she looked at his chin, noticing the peach fuzz that had made him so proud several months earlier. How he brushed out that fuzz as if he could produce a better, thicker beard by magic. She had teased him mercilessly about it but now it was the very thing that magnified the situation.

The truth was that he was still a child, and so was she. Maybe if they had a few more years to grow up they could have made this work, and it might have been beautiful. But they didn't have a few more years. What they had was right here and now, and as it stood, they were barely more than children.

"We can't do this, Jase. We don't have anywhere we call home, no way to pay the bills, and no guarantee of any kind of future. She deserves better than that, doesn't she?" Ali's voice cracked on the last word as she hugged Rose tightly to her chest. She breathed in the smell of her sweet skin and softly kissed the top of her head.

"What she deserves is having her parents with her. What she deserves is not being ripped away from the first people she's ever loved. What she *deserves* is not to have to struggle with her identity for the rest of her life." His voice was rising.

"I know that's *your* story, but maybe it won't be hers," she snapped again. Then added more softly, "All I know is that we can't do this. Not together, and not alone. We have a lot more growing up to do, and we just don't have the time."

"Ali, please don't do this."

Out of the corner of her eye, she saw another flower petal fall to the table. The bustling sounds of the hospital just outside her room broke into her thoughts. The bursts of laughter as nurses gossiped together at their station, the squeaking shoes of visitors walking quickly to their destination, the rolling wheels of food carts. Most people out there would take their babies home. She envied them so much her chest began to burn. Every one of them was oblivious to the hearts breaking on the other side of her door. She smiled sadly as she finally looked up into his eyes.

"I'm so sorry but this is what's best...for all of us." The ache in her chest grew as tears began gently streaming down her cheeks. Jason opened his mouth to say something then shut it. His fists opened and closed, and his jaw clenched and unclenched as he ran his hand through his hair in frustration. He paced, muttering to himself, and after a few minutes turned to face her.

"Well, I'm not signing *my* rights away, Ali. You do what you want." He leaned over her and kissed the top of Rose's head.

Ali breathed in the familiar scent of his cologne and took a mental snapshot of the moment. She had a feeling she might never see him again. He slowly stood back up, grabbed his jacket off the back of the chair, and moved toward the door. He stopped just before walking out, turned to look at them once more, then left.

Ali let out her breath the moment he was out of sight. The nurse looked over sympathetically and slowly came toward her.

"You're doing the right thing, hon," she said soothingly.

"Then why does it hurt so much?" Ali swallowed down a sob. She clutched her chest and bent over while she focused on breathing in and out. She buried her face into Rose's dark curls and breathed her in deeply. It was true what they said about the heads of babies. The smell was intoxicating, even on a brand-new child. She cradled her in her arms and stared at her face, committing it to memory. She began to sing a lullaby her mother used to sing to her as a child.

Sleep now, sweet baby
Your mommy's right here
Just close your eyes
For I'll always be near
All of your dreams will be
Safe from now on
Remember you're loved
While I sing you this song

Her voice cracked on the last word and she choked back the sobs that threatened to consume her, kissed Rose's cheek, and motioned for the nurse to take her.

"You shouldn't leave so soon." The woman's eyes were full of sympathy.

Ali shook her head slightly, took her clothes to the bathroom, and slowly got dressed. The stitches pulled, but that wasn't the worst pain—or her biggest fear. She caught a glimpse of herself in the mirror and took a moment to splash her face with some cold water. Her eyes stung with the threat of fresh tears, but she gripped the sides of the sink and forced them back. After a few gulps of air, she knew she was as ready as she was ever going to be. She exited the bathroom slowly and saw that the nurse had placed Rose in a crib beside the bed. She didn't lean down into the crib to kiss her or even look at her. She had done that already.

Instead, she took the envelope from the side table. It looked fat with pages inside—pages she would not read because she knew she wouldn't understand what they said. She only went to the last page; her parents' signatures were already there, waiting. Her mother's signature looked perfect, her father's was barely legible as always.

Her own name looked strange to her, like any word does after it's been read too many times. Ali, Ali, Ali. What did any of it mean? She didn't know, but she signed. The pen left a blue smudge on her finger, but she didn't wipe it.

She grabbed the rest of her belongings, and her neck prickled because she would not turn back once more. The nurse had been sorry, yet she was already bustling around, doing her job. Erasing Ali from the room. She would take Rose somewhere soon, where she would be picked up like a package.

In the hallway, Ali fell into step behind a nervous-looking man holding a bunch of pink balloons with the words, "It's a girl!" waving side to side in front of her. Only a few feet away from the room, and it had felt like miles, she heard the sound of her daughter's cries. The elevator opened fast and hard, wobbling a little as if saying, "In or out, make your choice!"

Once she was down on the ground floor and then outside in the fading sunlight, she looked around and saw her mother's shiny black car waiting for her. She headed toward it.

Wordlessly, she got into the back and closed the door. As soon as her seatbelt was buckled, her mother drove away from the curb. The hospital was only in the rear-view mirror now. She couldn't bring herself to look away as she watched it get smaller and smaller and smaller until it vanished completely from her sight.

It was behind her now, the hospital and this chapter of her life, and she would move on. She would suffer—she could feel it the way you could feel electricity in the air before a storm—but she'd survive this; she had no other choice.

And maybe she did, but this isn't her story: it's mine.

1

Name:

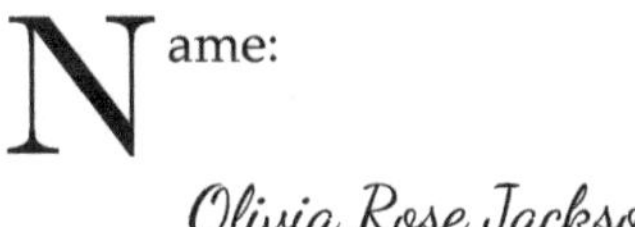

Age:

16

Family History of Illnesses:

Adopted.

I was so tired of filling out medical forms. How many times in my life was I going to have to tell someone that I had no idea what my medical history was? Well, half of it anyway. I sighed loudly in frustration. The sound caused the receptionist to glance up at me from her computer screen, so I smiled sweetly at her. No need to cause a scene.

She went back to typing on her computer while I stared vacantly at her gray hair and tired eyes. She had on a pale green blouse with puffy shoulders that made her look straight out of 1985. Who was she anyway? Where was Anne? Why did I even need to fill this form out? I'd been coming here for ages. Maybe something was wrong. Maybe they'd lost my files and I'd be made to remember every single appointment I'd ever had.

My palms were sweating.

Or maybe they just needed to update their files. *Stop freaking out, Liv,* I scolded myself.

I fidgeted in my seat and looked around the brightly lit room, taking in the fresh cream-colored paint on the walls and the circular pattern in the drop ceiling. It looked like a sterile environment that they tried to warm up with a softer shade of white. Somehow, it had always worked for me.

There was no art in the room except for the sole picture of a woman looking entirely too happy with her herpes diagnosis. The words "1 in 6 people between the ages of 15 to 49 suffer from genital herpes. Start Valtrex now so you don't have to" were written below her smiling face. I snorted to myself and shifted in the hard plastic chair for the hundredth time. Trying to find a comfortable position in it was impossible.

The plain ballpoint pen I was holding had been poised over the form in front of me for almost five minutes. I looked around the room again. There was a woman busily scratching away at her papers. She was an older, heavyset lady who looked like the neighborhood grandmother. She peered up and smiled when our eyes met. I smiled shyly and looked down feigning interest in the form I was no closer to filling out. Why couldn't they have just copied my information over? It's not like I was a stranger here.

I gave up, popped up out of my seat, and walked over to the single windowed reception area to hand it in. The receptionist glanced at it quickly and looked up at me with one eyebrow raised so high on her forehead I was sure it was going to fly right off. I tried not to laugh and had to look away to compose myself. *Pull it together, Liv!*

"Olivia Rose Jackson?" she said in a high, screechy voice as she surveyed the form. The eyebrow climbed a little higher. "No medical history?"

The familiar pull in my stomach tightened at her words. Her tone didn't bother me as much as the flat, disapproving stare.

I took a deep breath.

"Umm no, I was adopted." I glanced at the form to highlight the fact that it was written there, in front of her. She looked at it and pursed her lips.

"But your real parents didn't give your new ones their family history?" she demanded impatiently. This woman had no idea how sealed up adoption records can be. I just stared at her with my eyebrows raised to match hers. Someone who had seen too many patients in her lifetime, I guessed.

"Very well then, I'll call you when it's your turn." She dismissed me with an airy wave of her hand.

Back in my seat, I went through the motions of flipping through a magazine. I glanced at the large NO CELL PHONES sign on the wall for the third time, and even though I could feel my phone buzzing in my pocket, I was a rule-follower, so I ignored it. I knew it was probably Mela anyway.

Mela, short for Carmella, and I had crawled to each other as toddlers in a playgroup, or so the story went. We'd been friends ever since and our moms too, which was kind of cool. I mean, as cool as your mom being friends with your best friend's mom can get.

"Olivia Jackson?" I jumped a little at the sound of my name and quickly got up from the stiff plastic chair.

Grandma Betty (I had decided that was the name of the woman before me), had already gone in for her appointment and I was at a loss as to why the receptionist felt it necessary to say my name like a question. I fumbled with the magazine while trying to put it back and dropped it three times before slamming it down on the small table. I was too busy being frustrated with my clumsiness to notice that the receptionist had moved, and I walked straight into her. She motioned for me to follow her down the hall with a heavy eye roll. This woman loved her job.

I followed her into a small examination room crammed with two chairs, a computer desk, a rolling stool, an examination table, and the same bright beige paint on the walls. She typed some things into the computer and told me the doctor would be right in. As soon as she left the room, I snuck my cell phone out and peeked at it quickly. Nine texts from four different people, and five of them were from Mela.

I began to respond but the door started opening. I hurriedly threw my phone into my purse just as the doctor walked in.

"Hi, I'm Dr. Teagen." He introduced himself.

I stared at him blankly. He didn't look much older than I was. He politely pretended not to notice my surprise.

"What happened to Dr. Bowles?" I asked incredulously.

Dr. Bowles had been my doctor since I was adopted. He had white hair and kind eyes that twinkled when he smiled. This guy was like twenty-something, with short brown hair and brown eyes. He looked like he spent a lot of time at the gym and probably had had braces at some point because his teeth were ridiculously straight. What could he possibly know about doctoring? Was that a *word*? I wasn't sure.

"He retired a few months ago and I took over his patients," he replied pleasantly.

"Huh," I snorted flatly.

"You're Olivia Jackson?" he asked while looking at the chart I had just filled out.

"Yeah," I muttered.

"And you're adopted?" He sounded surprised.

"Uh-huh."

"You're my first adopted patient." He gave me a smile.

"Huh," I said again.

Wow, I was on fire. What I needed was for the floor to open up and swallow me whole. I didn't even know why I cared so much that I had a new doctor. To most people, it wouldn't have been a big deal, but I wasn't most people. *Just chill*, I told myself, *this isn't worth freaking out over*. If only my racing heart would catch up to my words.

"What brings you in?" he asked politely.

I was sure I could see a hint of amusement in his eyes. I was now positive the staff was going to sit around later and casually discuss the bumbling idiot that had graced them with her presence that day. I realized that he was still waiting for an answer, so I put the brakes on my paranoia and told him why I was there.

"I'm on the track team at Gibbons High, and all athletes need to have a physical done." Finally, a coherent sentence.

"Are you any good?" he asked as he turned the stool and started typing into his computer.

"Yeah, I'm okay," I mumbled. I didn't like to brag. The fact was that I was better than okay. I had a room full of ribbons and medals to prove it, but I didn't run to win; I ran to escape.

Dr. Teagen asked me to jump up onto the examination table. He proceeded to bring me a little stool to help me climb up after noticing how tall I wasn't; I still struggled. Once I was up there, he listened to my lungs through his stethoscope as I took deep breaths. I tried to look elsewhere. I had always found it awkward to stare someone in the eyes. I focused on a chip in the otherwise perfect wall. I glanced down at my chart reading and re-reading the words written about me while he took my blood pressure: bi-racial, green eyes, dark brown hair, 120lbs, 5" 1 & ½'…

I smirked at the added half-inch on the chart. Every bit counts when you're short.

He finished the rest of the physical and told me I was the picture of health, whatever that meant. I thanked him, got my medical permission slip signed for school, and left. Mela had dropped me off at the clinic, and since I wasn't far from home I decided to walk.

It was a beautiful sunny mid-September day in Fort Lauderdale. Palm trees and flowers were everywhere. I was comfortable in black shorts and a red tank top as I strolled down the cement sidewalk on my way home. I passed by funky colored hotels and beach shops along the boulevard. The wind blew the familiar scent of salty ocean air mixed with tacos toward me, and I breathed it in deeply. Most of the tourists had made a mass exodus a few weeks earlier, and mainly locals were left behind. I watched as couples rollerbladed down the street together holding hands, as joggers waved to their favorite street vendors, and as little kids licked melting ice cream cones. I smiled at the way the wind caressed my face like a warm hug.

I felt my phone buzz in my pocket. I pulled it out and glanced at the call display. I hit accept and put the phone to my ear.

"HEY, CHRIS!" I said.

"Hey, where are you?" He sounded irritated.

"I had a doctor's appointment, remember?"

"Huh, no I guess I forgot. I swung by to pick you up after school, but you weren't there. Where are you now? It sounds like you're walking."

"I'm just heading home."

"I'll come to get you." I heard the sound of his engine revving.

"It's my night to make dinner, so…" I trailed off. I tried not to sound annoyed that he'd just assumed I'd drop everything to be with him.

"What's going on, Liv?"

"Nothing!" There was such a long stretch of silence that I

looked at my phone to see if we were still connected. I heard him sigh.

"I'm sorry!" I blurted out immediately. Why did I always do that?

"Yeah, me too. I was looking forward to seeing you today." He sounded both stern and disappointed.

"I'm sorry," I mumbled again, feeling badly for letting him down.

"It's fine," he said, too fast, and after a moment added more brightly, "I'll see you tomorrow night for our anniversary dinner. Pick you up at seven?"

"Yeah, of course. Can't wait."

"I love you, babe."

"You too."

I smiled to myself at the thought of a three-month anniversary dinner. I had never celebrated such a random accomplishment, but I supposed most girls would be happy their boyfriends remembered. My phone buzzed again.

Still alive, or do I need to replace you?

I snorted at Mela's text then wrote back.

Still alive, guess you're stuck with me for now.

I could see she was writing again.

Blah, too bad for me. See you in the morning then.

I laughed and rolled my eyes as I tucked my phone away and headed home. It was nice to have such a caring friend, I thought to myself sarcastically as I put in my earbuds and enjoyed the sun on my face. It was almost the weekend, and I was determined to make it a good one.

2

I rushed into homeroom just as the second bell went off. I took my seat in the back row and avoided Mr. Koffra's disapproving glare.

"Third time this week, Olivia." His stern voice made me shrink down into my seat.

"Sorry, Mr. Koffra," I mumbled.

"Well, if that were true, you'd be on time more often."

He pushed his spectacles back up his oversized nose and clicked his tongue. My face felt hot as snickers filled the brightly lit room. I looked away and caught Mela's eye as she rolled her eyes dramatically and shook her head from side to side. I didn't dare smile; Mr. Koffra was still looking my way.

Mercifully he released me from his gaze and began roll call. I pulled out my unfinished homework and started scribbling the answers as fast as I could. I really needed to start finishing my homework at home. Katie Bryan laughed loudly with her minions beside me, and I looked up, waiting for her to be chastised. That never happened. Mr. Koffra simply relaxed into his chair with his daily Sudoku and ignored her completely.

Must be nice to be rich in this place, I muttered to myself.

The bell rang just then, and I got up quickly to shuffle out with the rest. The familiar beige and blue hallways were cluttered with students, and the smell of bacon wafting from the cafeteria filled my nostrils. Row upon row of gray lockers stretched before me; the only difference between them were their numbers and differently colored locks. Mela quickly caught up to me and linked her arm with mine. I pulled away uncomfortably and adjusted my backpack.

"Late again, Liv?" she asked breezily.

"Technically, I was exactly on time," I replied with a sheepish grin.

"Uh-huh. So, what are we doing tonight?" The words hung awkwardly in the air as we walked to class.

Finally, I said, "Uh… I have that anniversary thing with Chris tonight. Three months!" I held up three fingers.

"You know that's ridiculous, right?" It wasn't a question.

"You wouldn't be saying that if you'd ever made it to three months with a guy." I immediately regretted the words as I caught the hurt look in her eyes.

"It's just that we haven't spent much time together since I moved back," she said quietly. "Chris never wants to double-date with us. He just keeps you all to himself."

I smiled sympathetically and stopped at the end of the hallway. Turning to look at her, I was struck again by how much we looked alike. Same height, same color of hair, and even our mannerisms were similar. For example, the way she was now standing with her arms folded, tapping her foot impatiently.

"I'm sorry, Mel. I just…I like him." I looked down at the painted floor, noticing every pair of shoes that squeaked by.

"Yeah, well, maybe I would too if I ever spent any time with him. Whatever, just text me later 'k? I miss you." I looked up as she smiled sadly at me.

I nodded and hugged my arms across my chest.

"I miss you too," I mumbled to myself as we parted ways down separate corridors.

"ON YOUR MARKS, GET SET, GO!"

Coach Stewart clapped his hands, and I took off like a rocket.

I loved track practice; it was my favorite part of the day. My feet pounded against the red rubber track, my arms pumped me forward, and the wind pushed on my face as I ran. I breathed in deeply the familiar scent of the heated rubber of the track mixed with freshly cut grass from the football field. My thigh muscles burned as I pushed them to their breaking point.

"Pace yourself, Jackson!" Coach Stewart warned from the field as I pulled farther ahead of everyone else on the straightaway. The four-hundred-meter race was a brutal one. There was no pacing yourself, in my opinion. There just wasn't time for it. If I slowed down, I risked someone gaining on me.

I thought of Mela's face earlier and winced. She had looked so sad, and I knew she was right. I had hardly spent any time with her since I'd started dating Chris. Maybe I could ask him to make an exception and go on a double date.

The thought was immediately rejected. He'd never go for that, and I didn't want him to lump me in with other sixteen-year-olds. He was always telling me how mature I was.

Breathing too quickly, I forced myself to inhale slowly and deeply as I leaned into the corner of the track, making sure to stay within the white lines of my lane. I was still way ahead of everyone else in lane five, right in the middle of the track where I liked it best. The outside lane was too misleading; it could make you think you were ahead when you were not, and then the runner on the inside lane could shoot past you at the last second.

The middle was exactly where I liked to be.

As soon as I rounded the bend, I flew into the last straightaway and pushed myself even harder. My arms and legs were pumping in unison. Left arm up, right leg up. Right arm up, left leg up. The only sounds I could hear were the wind rushing through my ears and my feet thudding against the track. I didn't bother to look back to see where anyone else was. I never saw the point of that. The only person I competed with was myself.

At less than fifty meters left I gave it all I had. Most people were done at this point of the race, but I liked to turn it up even more, finding strength and resolve when I didn't think I had any left. The only part of me hitting the ground were the balls of my feet. I flew across the finish line and leaned into it like I always did. *Leave it all on the track*. That's what every coach I'd ever had told me, and so that's what I did.

I slowed my pace to a jog and turned around when I was about to round the corner of the track. The rest of the runners were just crossing the finish line as I walked back. My legs felt like Jell-O, and there was a stitch in my side so bad that I had to lift my arm above my head and try to touch the opposite shoulder to stretch it out.

"Coach Stewart, this is supposed to be cross country, not sprinting," Melanie Carmichael complained loudly while trying to catch her breath by leaning down on her knees. Her strawberry blonde hair was a frizzy mess, half in her ponytail and half out.

He looked over at me and winked with a twinkle in his blue eyes. His white hair was blowing in the wind as he zipped up his matching black and white track suit. I looked away quickly, before Melanie could see the smirk on my face. Coach Stewart was the cross-country and track-&-field coach, but he and I preferred track, much to the frustration of all the cross-country runners.

"You're right, Melanie. Why don't you go ahead and run a couple of laps to cool down?"

She scoffed in disbelief, silently strode past him, and began a slow jog.

"Everyone, go ahead and join Melanie for the cool down and then we'll call it a day," he called out cheerfully. We all followed, and just as I was about to start running, he waved me over. He waited until everyone was out of earshot to speak.

"Olivia, I have some good news." The smile on his face was contagious.

"What is it?" I asked excitedly.

"A scout is coming out to the track meet in a few months once the season 'officially' starts, and he's planning to offer you a spot on the Lion's Track Club." My jaw dropped. The Lion's Track Club was an elite track team which only the best of the best got invited to join. Many of the athletes who were a part of it went on to compete in the Olympics eventually.

"Are you serious?" I squealed.

"Yes, ma'am!" He gave me a high five. "Just keep doing what you're doing, and you'll be a shoo-in. I'm proud of you."

He smiled and nodded toward the track. I beamed at him and began my cool down. I could hardly believe it, and I couldn't wait to tell Mela. All of those grueling practices and meets had finally paid off. I felt like the luckiest girl in the world, and I wasn't sure if I'd ever stop smiling.

3

After practice, I walked home a little more slowly than usual. I was still really excited about what Coach Stewart had told me, but the happiness I was feeling kept fading whenever I thought about my date with Chris. I took the familiar path along the water and let out the breath I was holding as soon as I could see the ocean. Checking the time, I saw that I only had a couple of hours before Chris picked me up. My phone buzzed with a text from Mela.

Amazing about the Lion's Club! Not surprised, though, you're the best runner I've ever seen. And...sorry about earlier. If you're happy I'm happy.

I read and re-read the text. *"If you're happy I'm happy"* kept replaying in my mind.

Thanks, babe.

I put my phone away and pursed my lips as I walked. *Was I happy*? I asked myself. *I wasn't unhappy*... I shrugged.

There was a growing unease in the pit of my stomach; I immediately stuffed it down. *It'll be fine, Liv, fun even. It's just a three-month anniversary, it's not like you're marrying the guy. Don't let this ruin the news you just got.*

There, that felt better. I nodded to myself and picked up the pace.

As my house came into view, I cringed at the purple garage. My dad had recently painted it and I still wasn't sure if he did it because my mom asked him to or because it was against the city by-laws. Either way, as I walked up the driveway, I sheepishly waved to the neighbor across the street, who was glaring toward our house. He didn't wave back.

And as soon as I walked in the door, I nearly tripped on size-twelve Birkenstocks carelessly lying in the middle of the hallway. I immediately knew that my sister was visiting. *Great,* I thought, *this should be awkward, as usual.* I placed my shoes beside hers, took a deep breath, and forced a smile on my face as I walked toward the laughter that had just erupted in the kitchen.

My sister leaned against the pale green counter, sloshing her ice water while telling my mom a story. I took off my backpack and sat down quietly at the kitchen table, not wanting to interrupt. I wanted to tell them about the Lion's Club, but their response was always so underwhelming that I found myself hesitating.

"Hey, Liv, try to turn down the volume next time you come in. I could barely hear myself think." My sister's sarcasm was on point as usual.

"Hilarious, Amanda." I matched her tone.

I grabbed my math homework and started scratching the answers down; I really didn't want a repeat of this morning, so I figured I'd better get my homework done now. My sister kept chatting with my mom, and every now and then I'd glance up and smile or politely comment.

Covertly, I studied my sister, trying to figure out why she looked so different. Her short hair was dyed blonde today and styled in a pixie cut. My eyes were drawn to her bright red lipstick and square, black-rimmed glasses. Somehow, she made glasses look cool. I still couldn't figure out what was making her seem off though.

"Liv, honey, could you clear your stuff off the table, please? We'll be eating dinner soon." My mom's voice was soft and soothing as always. I nodded and began packing my homework away as she shuffled by me with plates and utensils. She was still wearing her work clothes: gray slacks, collared white button-up shirt, no jewelry or makeup.

"So, Liv! What's going on?" my sister asked as she crunched loudly on a piece of ice.

"Not too much, Amanda. How's apartment life?" I inquired dutifully.

"Aaaaamazing! I absolutely love living downtown. Last week my roommate and I threw a party. A PARTY! Can you believe it?" I opened my mouth to answer but she continued. "Then someone broke my glasses, but I was able to snag this pair, which I totally love, but they were SO expensive! And I got colored contacts. Now I have blue eyes."

That's what the difference was! I nearly snapped my fingers but contained myself.

"You're wearing glasses *and* contacts? Overdoing it a little, aren't you?" I asked with a grimace.

"Yeah, they didn't have my prescription, so these contacts are just for show. We can't all have green eyes and perfect eyesight like you. Some of us were actually *born* into this family." She said it casually as she walked over to the table and put her glass down.

"Lucky me," I mumbled quietly.

"I'm going to go change before your dad gets home, okay girls? It's nice to have you home for a meal, Amanda." My mom squeezed her arm as she walked by and headed to her room to change.

Amanda brushed past me and sat on the living room couch

my parents had recently bought at a garage sale. Beige with pink and blue swirls that matched nothing in the house—kind of like me. They were thrilled.

"So…how's—uhh—soccer is it?" she asked as she scratched her head.

"Track, actually," I mumbled as I came and sat stiffly on the dark brown 70's recliner across from her.

"Oh, right, right, right," she muttered distractedly as she pulled out her phone.

My dad walked through the front door, and his head peered into the living room at us.

"Amanda, what a…surprise." He smiled civilly then turned to me. "Hey, kiddo!" His tone was much warmer, making me cringe internally. Did he have to make it so obvious that he and I were closer than they were?

"Hey, Dad," Amanda and I said in unison.

"Where's your mother?" he asked, even as he headed towards their room, not waiting for an answer.

I avoided returning the gaze I could feel my sister throwing my way. Soon my parents came downstairs, laughing about something, while my mom lovingly swatted at my dad in mock annoyance. He sniffed the air appreciatively.

"Is dinner ready?" he asked.

"Yes, let's eat!" my sister said quickly.

We stood up at the same time, and she strode by me. My dad pulled me into a hug, and I wrapped my arms around him and pressed my head against his chest just above his stomach. He playfully rubbed my hair and pulled away. I watched him gallop into the kitchen with his long legs and thin build. His salt-and-pepper hair had dirt in it, as it usually did after work.

"Whose house did you fix today, Dad?" Amanda asked casually.

He immediately rolled his eyes and sighed dramatically. "Mrs. Cooper's; *again*. Do you know she called me to change a light bulb last week? Today she needed me to get rid of some critters in her attic."

My dad went on recounting his day as I quietly picked at my food. Vegetarian "meatloaf" tonight. I honestly didn't understand why we all had to stick to a vegetarian diet when it was just my mom who didn't eat meat anymore. Although, she *was* the one making the food, so I figured I didn't have much of a right to complain.

I listened as they all spoke over each other, trying to simultaneously get the first and last word in. I wondered sometimes if they were even listening to what the other person was saying or just waiting to speak again. I watched my dad and sister sitting there, unaware of how much they resembled each other. Both tall in stature, both with a commanding presence, the same jutting out of the chin, and playful smiles no one could resist. I looked like a foreigner sitting with them.

My dad's voice broke into my thoughts. "Not hungry, kiddo?"

"I need to save my appetite. I'm going on that date with Chris tonight." My voice sounded like a whisper in comparison.

"Oh, right!" He snapped his fingers.

"Be home by ten, please," my mom said quietly.

"*Ten*?" my sister demanded. "When I was her age my curfew was nine!" She looked incredulous.

"It's not like you ever showed up by curfew, Amanda."

My dad's words seemed to reverberate through the silence that followed. I stared hard at my plate, willing it to transform into a wormhole that would take me anywhere else.

"How was your day, dear?" My dad asked my mom between bites.

"Oh, the usual. Putting other people's fires out, handling the most irate customers, adding up a million bills." She smiled, but the circles under her eyes and the way they no longer shone betrayed her; she was worn out.

"Amazing, I didn't realize the phone company was so thrilling," Amanda said with a forced laugh.

I picked at my plate for a few more minutes and glanced nervously at the clock. I was running out of time.

"May I be excused to go get ready, please?" I asked politely.

"You may," my parents answered in unison. I cleared my plate from the table and headed toward my room.

"Ten, Liv," my mom called after me.

"Got it, Mom!" I called back as I raced downstairs to shower, get changed and put on my makeup.

Chris hadn't told me where we were going, and I wasn't sure what to wear. I settled on jeans and a turquoise tank top to match my eyes. I wore my gold locket as usual, and some small, gold hoop earrings. I put my hair half up the way he liked it, gave myself a last once over in the mirror, and headed upstairs.

"So, who are you going out with?" Amanda's voice came from behind me as I was putting my flats on.

"His name is Chris," I said casually inching toward the door.

"Chris who?" Her eyes narrowed slightly.

"You probably wouldn't know him." My hand was on the door handle.

"Try me." She folded her arms across her chest.

I sighed. "Chris Jamieson," I said quietly.

Her eyebrows raised and she stepped closer to me.

"Isn't he like twice your age?"

"Of course not! He's only twenty-two," I said defensively.

"May as well be twice your age, Liv. What's he doing with a sixteen-year-old?" She didn't mask the disapproval in her voice.

"I'm almost seventeen," I mumbled.

"Right." She stared at me. "Do Mom and Dad know?"

"Not exactly." I wasn't sure if she was going to rat me out or not.

She let her arms drop and sighed. "Look, you covered for me a bunch when I still lived here, so I'll do you this solid. But be careful. I know we don't always get along, but you're my sister."

My throat tightened at her words, and I simply nodded. She gave me one last look and walked back to the kitchen, shaking her head. I let out a shaky breath and walked out the door before she had time to change her mind.

4

I waited nervously under the palm tree at the end of my driveway. I could hear the bass before seeing Chris's black Camaro. He pulled up at exactly seven, and I hopped in his car quickly. My parents weren't huge fans of loud music and showy cars. I saw my dad peek his head out from behind the living room curtain with a disapproving glare. I cringed down in my seat.

Chris said nothing as he pulled away from my house. I glanced shyly at him and saw that he was dressed in well-pressed brown shorts with a dark belt, a white polo shirt, and a dark blue sweater tied loosely around his neck. I could smell the familiar scent of his body wash mixed with cologne. His brown hair was styled with gel, and he was clean-shaven. His blue eyes were hidden behind his aviator sunglasses, so I couldn't read his expression. The silence stretched on between us until I finally broke it.

"You okay?" I shouted over the music. I couldn't put my finger on it, but I felt like something was off. He turned the music down and sighed heavily in response. I looked out the window, watching the trees fly by, and waited for him to speak.

"I don't think we see tonight the same way, that's all," he said quietly. I racked my brain, trying to think of what that cryptic sentence could mean, but I was at a loss. Until we pulled up to the restaurant, that is. *Crap*. We were at Bernard's.

Bernard's was the kind of place you needed to book at least a month out. I had only ever been once as a kid, when my grandmother died. I looked down at my jeans and tank top and immediately regretted my wardrobe choice.

"I'm sorry, I didn't realize…" I trailed off.

"That's okay. Let's just make the best of it. I've been looking forward to this for a while." He turned and smiled at me, and I felt my stomach flutter.

"Me too," I whispered shyly. I still wasn't entirely sure why he was with me, but it felt nice to be chosen.

I leaned over and quickly kissed his cheek. His smile widened, and he parked the car. We got out, and as we walked toward the restaurant, he pulled my hand into his. It was soft and smooth, not like my dad's rough hands, but I held it the same way.

We approached the door for the maître d' to look me up and down. I shrank back a little behind Chris. The man reluctantly waved us through after checking our reservation. A perky hostess introduced herself as Crystal and motioned for us to follow her to our table. As we walked through the restaurant, I felt completely out of place. Light piano music was playing softly in the background and the tables were set in white tablecloths, with crisp white napkins holding more cutlery than seemed necessary. Candlelight flickered between each couple and fresh roses in crystal vases stood at every table. The lights were dimmed, which gave everything a romantic feel. The hostess brought us to our table, which was in a secluded part of the restaurant. As we both sat down, she let us know that our waitress would be right with us. My phone started buzzing and I pulled it out to see who it was, but as I caught the look on Chris's face, I quickly threw it back into my purse.

His face smoothed over and he reached across the table for my hand.

"How was your day?" he asked softly.

"Just the usual. School, homework, you know, that sort of thing. My sister came."

His eyes seemed to darken for just a second, but he recovered so quickly that I wasn't sure if I had just imagined it in the dim lighting.

"Alana, right?" he asked as he took a sip of water.

"Amanda," I corrected him.

He nodded.

"How do you know her again?" I asked as if I knew the answer.

"I don't." he cleared his throat and changed the subject. "I was talking to Kyle again today at work."

"You're his boss, right?"

"Something like that." He smirked as though I had missed the punch line of a joke. I was still in the dark about what he did for work. Something to do with computers, and he had explained it enough times that I should really know it by now.

"Anyway, his girlfriend is a bit younger than he is too, but she's always nagging him to hang out with her friends. I told him that *my* girlfriend was much more mature than that and never bothered me with that trivial stuff." He smiled at me. I was instantly glad that I had decided not to ask him about going on a double date with Mela and Nate. Although I realized that he was in fact calling my best friend "trivial stuff." I wasn't sure how I felt about that.

The waitress came up to our table.

"Hi there, I'm Amber. I'll be your waitress tonight. Can I get you started with something to drink?" Her red ponytail bobbed as she cocked her head to the side, waiting for our answers.

"I'll have a beer"—Chris motioned toward me—"and she'll have a sparkling water."

I hated sparkling water, yet I kept quiet.

"Sure thing," she said as she handed each of us a single sheet menu. "Our specials are—"

Chris interrupted without looking at her. "Just the drinks, for now, thanks."

She raised her eyebrow and looked questioningly at me. I gave her a half-smile and shrugged my shoulders apologetically as she turned and walked away. I hated when he did that, but it was nice that he only had eyes for me. I looked around the restaurant and noticed the performer at the grand piano off to the side. An elderly couple moved on the dance floor, and I smiled as I watched them slowly twirl. It was clear they had been doing this dance for years, the way they moved in synchronicity together.

"Do you want to dance?" I hadn't noticed Chris watching me. Heat flooded my face immediately.

"No, no that's okay." I took a nervous sip of water. He stood up and stretched his hand toward me.

"Come on, Olivia, dance with me."

Hesitantly, I put my hand in his and let him pull me up. I followed him slowly to the dance floor. He pulled me close, and I stiffened in his arms.

"Relax," he murmured quietly into my ear. I took a deep breath and forced myself to loosen up and sway to the music with him. He put one arm around my waist and held my other hand. I felt like everyone was watching us, so I stared at his shoulder intently.

"Do you remember the day we met?" he whispered.

"I do," I whispered back.

"The moment I saw you at that bookstore, I knew I had to have you."

"Really?" I asked thoughtfully.

"Of course, I thought you were much older then. You just had this way about you. I couldn't take my eyes off you." His words made me smile.

I hadn't even noticed him that day, but suddenly he had been right there asking me a million questions about myself and telling me how beautiful I was. It was hard to resist that kind of flattery. The song came to an end and he kissed my forehead before leading me back to our table. Our drinks had arrived, as well as a basket full of delightfully smelling rolls and fresh butter in the shape of a heart. I waited for him to grab a roll and followed suit, taking little nibbles of it here and there. I could feel him watching me, so I glanced up quickly and made eye contact for a second before looking away again.

"You would look so good in a dress. You should wear them more often."

"I'm not really a dress girl," I said with a laugh. I could feel him staring at me until I looked back.

"Not even for me?" he asked softly.

I cleared my throat. "I mean, I guess I could start…" I trailed off, annoyed with myself for agreeing to something I didn't want to do. I hate dresses, I told myself. *But I guess I hate saying no more than I hate dresses.*

He sat back in his chair triumphantly. "I look forward to seeing you in one."

I smiled quickly and nodded. *Great, guess I'm going dress-shopping this weekend. Mela will be thrilled.* The waitress came back to our table and took our orders. Or rather, took Chris's version of our orders. I hadn't really wanted a salad, but apparently that's what I was having.

"My coach told me that a scout is coming to watch me run at the next track meet in the spring," I mentioned casually. I was bursting to tell someone other than Mela.

"What does that mean?" His eyes narrowed slightly.

"I guess he's planning to offer me a spot on the Lion's Track Team, which consists of the best of the best runners in the city," I proudly explained.

He smiled stiffly and seemed confused. "So, you'll be part of *two* track teams?"

"Umm, yeah, I guess so. The Lions practice in the evenings and on weekends, so I'll have time for both."

"But no time for me, I guess." His eyes darkened.

"I'd still make time for you, Chris," I mumbled and felt my shoulders slump.

"We'll see." He smiled. "That's great, though. I'm sure you're happy." He grabbed another roll to butter.

Well, I *was* happy, I thought to myself.

I excused myself to go to the restroom, and after getting lost twice I managed to find it twenty feet from our table. Elevator music was playing through the speakers, and as I washed my hands with the overpowering green-apple-scented soap, our waitress walked in behind me. I smiled at her in the reflection of the mirror and she walked over to the sink next to me and started washing her hands.

"Ugh, this soap smells nasty," she muttered.

"Right? Disgusting," I responded with a quick laugh.

"Honestly, it's like they stuffed a bushel of apples into this soap dispenser." I snorted as I grabbed some paper towels to dry my hands.

"What school do you go to?" she asked.

"I go to Gibbons."

"I went there. I graduated two years ago," she said as she shook the water from her hands.

"No way. I can't wait to get out of there," I said wistfully.

"Let me guess. Koffra for homeroom?" She laughed at the shocked expression on my face.

"Yes. He's the worst!" I cried.

"The worst," she agreed.

We laughed and headed toward the door. Before we walked out, she paused and cleared her throat—and as I looked up, her expression confused me. It was the same expression Mela always wore when she had to tell me something and didn't want to. My forehead creased automatically.

"I'm sorry, I really shouldn't say anything," she said.

"Is it my salad? It's gross, isn't it?" I knew it. *Who even puts pine nuts on a salad anyway?*

"Yeah, actually, it really is. What did *you* want to order?"

"Do you guys have burgers and fries?" I asked carefully. Nothing on the menu had looked very appealing to me. She laughed.

"I got you covered." She winked. Her hand on the door, she turned back to look at me.

"Be careful with guys like that. They're great…until they're not." She smiled sadly and left me standing there in the brightly lit restroom.

Where had that come from? I shook my head in an attempt to clear it and walked back to our table.

"You okay?" Chris asked suspiciously, looking up from his phone.

"What? Yeah, of course." I said it more enthusiastically than I felt. She was the third person to warn me about him *today*. I smiled at him and took a sip of my sparkling water. Yuck. He nodded his satisfaction and went back to his phone. The waitress came with our plates, and I grinned at the burger and fries in front of me. Chris was still looking at his phone, so he didn't notice my lack of salad. He had ordered salmon and steamed vegetables, no surprise there. Rarely did he let any kind of junk food pass his lips. He looked up from his phone and his smile faded.

"Didn't you order a salad?" he asked as he cut his vegetables with a fork and knife.

I felt a boldness come over me suddenly. "Well, actually *you* ordered a salad for me. *This* is what I really wanted."

I made a point to take a big bite of my burger as the asparagus speared on his fork froze halfway to his mouth.

"Okay…" he trailed off, then shook his head as though determined not to let this ruin our evening. The waitress popped in to see if we were enjoying our food.

"Delicious!" I said with a smirk. I saw her swallow a laugh.

"Can I actually get some plain water with lemon?" I asked.

"Of course! I'll bring that right over. Do you want me to just take this sparkling water away?" she asked.

"Yes please," I said, not missing Chris's raised eyebrows. As soon as she was gone, he looked right at me.

"What's gotten into you?" His eyes narrowed as he said it. The truth was I wasn't sure what had gotten into me, but I kind of liked it.

"What? Because I wanted a burger and fries over a salad?" I asked innocently.

"You're just not usually like this," he said quietly.

He was right; I was usually quiet and obedient—but it felt good to speak up even if it was just over a meal. I shrugged and took another bite of my burger. We finished our meals in silence and passed on dessert. I mouthed *thank you* to the waitress on our way out. I knew I hadn't seen burgers and fries on that fancy menu, so she must have pulled some strings. She nodded and smiled as we walked out the door.

It was only eight-thirty, and I was pondering what I'd do for the rest of the night as we drove. I figured I'd call Mela and make plans for tomorrow, since like she's said, we hadn't hung out all that much lately. Maybe I'd binge-watch a show or something. I was so distracted that I didn't immediately notice we weren't heading to my house.

"Where are we going?" I asked nervously.

"I have a surprise for you. Don't worry, I'll get you back by curfew."

He rolled his eyes playfully, but fear was pulling at the edges of my subconscious. I wasn't sure why I felt afraid. All I knew was that I did.

5

My palms were sweating, and I could feel my hands trembling slightly. What is wrong with me? Surprises aren't necessarily bad, I told myself. My attempts at self-soothing weren't working. I stared out the window, desperately looking for any clues as to where we were going. I could see we were heading downtown, and I was still in the dark until we pulled up to an apartment complex.

"I thought it was time you saw my place," he murmured gently.

My heart thudded furiously inside my chest and beads of sweat started to pool between my eyebrows. "Oh," I croaked in despair.

He pulled into a mostly empty parking lot and parked the car.

"You ready?" he asked with a smile.

My throat was so dry I didn't trust myself to speak, so I simply nodded. That seemed to be good enough for him. He got out and closed the door, while I sat frozen for what felt like an eternity. I didn't want to get out of the car, and panic began rising inside of me. Would he understand if I told him I just wanted to go home? Maybe, or maybe not.

A sudden knock at the window made me jump out of my skin. Chris was standing there, an impatient look on his face. I grabbed my purse with shaking hands and moved to get out, only to get slammed back into my seat by the seatbelt. He was still staring at me as I released the belt and opened the car door. I took in the faded brown building with small cement balconies lined up, one on top of the other. I counted fifteen floors before we walked through the front entrance.

I had been to a complex like this while visiting my aunt, but hers was much fancier and required a code to get in. Instead, we walked through a door that was barely hanging on by its hinges. The fluorescent lights flickered and hardly illuminated the gray, heavily stained carpet. Chris silently led me to one of two elevators and pushed the button. I was hoping beyond hope that his roommate Danny was home. I had met him a couple of times in passing when we were out to eat. I wasn't prepared to be alone with Chris in his apartment, and time was moving far too slowly for me to use my curfew as an excuse to leave.

A loud ding brought me back to reality as the elevator door wobbled open. I slowly followed Chris into the caged box, resisting the urge to slip out before the doors closed. I watched him push 4 and stared as the buttons lit up for each floor. Way too soon the elevator stopped, and the doors lurched open. I wondered whether he'd notice my absence if I just stayed behind.

I forced myself to step off the elevator and follow him down the hall lined with dark green walls and the same stained carpet. The paint was chipping badly and completely peeling in some spots. We came up to a white door with plenty of scuff marks and the numbers 517 painted on it. Chris fumbled with his keys and forced one into the lock roughly. He opened the door, and I walked in behind him. The apartment had large windows overlooking the city and at first glance seemed surprisingly clean.

"Do you want a tour?"

His voice caused me to jump slightly.

"Sure," I whispered as I slipped off my shoes.

I wanted to keep them on, but it seemed impolite to track dirt everywhere. We started in the kitchen with its bright white cabinets and black appliances. The double sink had one side full of clean dishes and a yellow cloth folded neatly over the other side. I followed him into the living room and noted the matching gray couches and oversized chair. There was even a cream-colored carpet on the floor.

"My sister helped us decorate," he said with a smile as I tried to mask my surprise.

We walked down the light-gray hall as he pointed out the single bathroom, his roommate's door, and his room right across from it.

"Do you want to come in?" He stood in the doorway, making room for me to get by.

I immediately saw a bed with a large blue comforter on it, and I involuntarily took a step back and shook my head slightly.

"No, I'm okay. It's a nice place." I volunteered as I made a point to look back toward the living room.

He sighed and clicked off the light to his room; I breathed a sigh of relief. This time I led the way back and sat in the oversized chair. He walked over to the television and grabbed the remote. He dimmed the lights and turned on a made-for-TV movie.

"I'll be right back," he purred.

Pushing down the shudder I felt rising in me, I just smiled tightly. I saw him go into the bathroom out of the corner of my eye and heard what sounded like an electric toothbrush turn on. Weird. After a couple of minutes, he was back to sit down on the couch across from me.

"Are you seriously going to sit all the way over there?" he asked, sounding offended.

After a silent internal fight, I stood up and walked over to the couch, sitting down beside him. He put his arm around me and immediately pulled me closer. I stiffened.

"Relax, Olivia," he murmured into my ear.

I squirmed in my seat. I didn't want to relax—I wanted to leave. Surely he didn't expect me to sleep with him tonight? I had no plans to lose my virginity any time soon, and a step like that would require a conversation at the very least. *Right?*

He turned my face toward his and with his eyes already closed leaned in and pressed his lips against mine. I tried to relax into his kiss, but I was painfully aware of every single noise around us. A commercial was playing loudly in the background: *"FOUR OUT OF 5 DENTISTS RECOMMEND..."* I had always wondered what the last dentist thought. Did he simply recommend something else? Or was he in total disagreement with the other four and was secretly planning a rebellion?

Chris's hand slid onto my stomach as he deepened the kiss. I flinched and pulled away.

"Come on, Olivia..." Again, he whispered into my ear as he kissed down the side of my face. His lips moved down to my neck, and I closed my eyes tightly, willing time to speed up.

"Chris, I need to get home soon," I stammered as I cleared my throat.

"There's still plenty of time. Just relax."

Once more I tried to protest, but his lips pressed against mine, more roughly this time. He leaned forward, and I found myself falling back into the couch as he pushed himself on top of me.

"Chris, no."

My voice was muffled by his lips, still pressed against mine. He parted them and shoved his tongue into my mouth. I tried to push him off, but that only made him press into me harder. My heart was beating furiously inside my chest as I continued to push against his shoulders. I felt his hand slide down and unbutton my jeans as I, now frantic, pushed him away.

Fear shot down my spine. He wasn't going to stop, and tears spilled onto my cheeks as he began pulling my pants down. I felt a scream bubble up into my throat; but it was muffled by his hand suddenly pressing over my mouth.

"Shhhh, you're fine. You don't need to be scared, it's going to feel amazing." His voice was ripe with excitement. The sound of his belt buckle being undone was like the sound of a whip. Then, the unmistakable hiss of his shorts unzipping as I sobbed into his hand and clawed at his shoulders.

"Don't worry, Olivia, you're going to love it. I've been dying to be your first."

His voice deepened with emotion as I thrashed beneath him, almost choking on my tears. He kissed my face again and again as he forced my knees up and I struggled beneath him.

"What the hell are you doing, man?"

The question came from the kitchen, and my eyes darted there to meet the shocked expression on his roommate's face. Chris sat up suddenly, as though he had been electrocuted.

"Danny! You said you wouldn't be home tonight," he shouted angrily.

"Plans changed," Danny said stiffly, taking a step toward us.

"We're fine here, bud. You can go."

Danny took another step forward.

"Doesn't look like it." He looked at my tear-stained face with concern.

I saw my opportunity and wasted no time. I rolled off the couch while simultaneously pulling my pants back up and ran toward the door.

"Olivia, wait!" Chris called out behind me.

Not a chance. I grabbed my purse and shoes and flew out of the apartment without closing the door. I ran straight past the elevator and yanked the door to the stairs open, jumping down three at a time. On the ground floor, I stumbled through the door and slammed straight into a robust woman wearing a red and white polka-dot dress.

"Excuse *me*!" Her hand flew up to her chest as she took several steps backward.

I flew straight out of the apartment building and into the dark of the night. I turned and headed toward the main road, still running in my socks at top speed. When I spotted a huge bush, I ran to it and crouched down while frantically searching through my purse for my phone. I grabbed it, stood up, and began to run again as I tried to dial Mela's number. My hands were shaking so badly and my eyes so blurry with tears that I kept pressing the wrong buttons.

Finally, I remembered that I had her on speed dial. Holding down the number two, I waited for it to start ringing. It only rang once before she picked up.

"Liv! You'll never guess what happened tonight."

As soon as I heard her voice, my chest was wracked with uncontrollable sobs.

"Liv? Liv? What's wrong?" she demanded.

I tried to speak, but I couldn't form any cohesive words. "I… I…" More sobs.

"Naaaaate," she screamed, muffling the phone. And to me, her voice shaking:

"Where are you? We'll come to get you."

"I…I can't…I…" More sobs.

"Let's just track her phone," Nate said in the background.

"Okay, Liv? We're gonna track your phone. Stay put, we'll be right there." I heard her shuffling quickly and stomping down the stairs.

"No!" I shrieked and immediately slammed my mouth shut, glancing from side to side. I wasn't about to sit still and wait for Chris to find me. I knew I had to keep moving.

"Alright," she said. "We'll find you. I'll stay on the phone with you okay?" I nodded even though she couldn't see me. She kept trying to ask me what had happened, so I tuned her out. I focused on the sound of my breathing and tried to steady it while I jogged. In, out. In, out. Left arm up, right leg up. Right arm up, left leg up. Someone was coming right behind me, and I whipped around as my heart jumped into my throat.

"Geez, chill out." It was a teenager walking her golden retriever. She flicked her cigarette and rolled her eyes as she crossed the path behind me and headed toward a park.

"Liv? Liv?" Mela's voice was screaming into my ear.

"Just...dog..." My teeth were chattering so hard, I could barely spit the words out. Funny, I didn't *feel* cold.

"Drive faster, Nate." Mela's tone was low and serious.

I continued to focus on my breathing as I kept going. The farther from Chris's place I got, the slower I ran until, finally, I was just walking. Having no idea where I was, I stayed close to the road. A vehicle pulled up beside me slowly.

"Get in the car, Olivia."

Ice shot through my veins as I heard Chris's cold voice coming from it. I took off immediately in the opposite direction he was driving. Fear flooded me as I gasped for breath. Someone was running behind me again, so I ran as fast as I could while Mela screamed my name through the phone in my ear.

My wrist was grabbed from behind and I whimpered in terror as I was turned around quickly. Headlights blinded me and made me blink hard as I tried to jerk my wrist away. I heard Chris call my name, only he sounded different. I kept trying to break free, but the grip simply tightened.

Suddenly Nate was in my face his blue eyes full of concern and his lips moving without sound. I blinked in confusion as I stared at his hand holding my wrist and followed his arm back up to his mouth, which was still moving. All I could hear was a high-pitched ringing in my ears as my eyes darted from side to side, attempting to make sense of my surroundings.

"Liv, holy crap are you okay?"

Nate's voice made me flinch. Mela ran up and pulled me into a tight hug. I stared down at her fuzzy pink sweater as tears continued to run down my face. That was her sleep sweater. She must have been heading to bed.

"It's okay, Nate," Mela told her boyfriend as she patted his hand to let go of my wrist. As soon as his grip loosened, I jerked my hand away and pulled it close to my side. Everything was coming in and out of focus as I tried to blink the confusion away.

Mela reached toward me slowly, as if I were a wild animal. I stared at her hand as it came closer to my face. She touched the phone still pressed up against my ear and gently pried my fingers from it. She used one hand to pull my phone away and the other to pry my shoes out of my other hand and pass them to Nate. She then tenderly led me toward his shiny black truck.

I climbed into the back wordlessly and sat as still as possible while Mela softly buckled my seat belt and sat beside me. When Nate closed the truck door, I jumped—and flinched as he walked around and got in the front. As soon as we pulled away, I fell apart and sobbed into Mela's shoulder. She rubbed my hair soothingly.

Nate kept nervously looking back at us through the rear-view mirror all the way back to Mela's house. I didn't even question the fact that we were there and not at my parents'. I walked numbly into the house, up the stairs, and flopped myself onto her queen-sized bed. Frantic, hushed whispers drifted up from the ground floor. It was a conversation between her and her parents. Then her mother was calling mine to say I was sleeping over. Her mom was cool like that.

Mela came upstairs, and I lay in her bed as she sat beside me softly rubbing my back. Every time I was close to falling asleep, I would jolt and gasp, and Mela would shush me back down with promises that it was all going to be okay. I knew she was wrong, though.

Nothing would ever be okay again.

6

I woke up groggily, trying to piece together where I was and why my clothes were still on. I rubbed my hand back and forth over the soft yellow comforter I was so used to and wondered why I was on top of it.

When I looked out the window, blinking at the sun, I got a flash of blinding headlights. The memories of the night before came rushing back and I sat up quickly with a gasp only to find Mela staring at me from her oversized leather chair across the room.

"*What* happened?" she asked with wide eyes full of concern. She was still wearing her fuzzy pink sweater and gray sweats. Cross-legged on the chair, she clutched a white throw pillow. The circles under her eyes were light purple, and worry lines creased her forehead. I sighed heavily as I lay back down covering my eyes with my arm.

"Liv, come on. You scared the crap out of us last night."

She got out of the chair and came my way, and I flinched when she touched my leg.

"What did he do?" she asked.

I swallowed hard and looked away as I cleared my throat. "Chris..." I began. I wasn't sure whether I wanted anyone to know what had happened; even Mela. Did I really need to tell anyone the details? I would just stay away from him and never be alone with any guy ever for the rest of my life. *There, problem solved,* I told myself, envisioning the plethora of cats I would have in my single bedroom apartment.

"What did he do?" she insisted.

I glanced at her. "He...he dumped me." My eyes betrayed me and filled with tears. Mela looked confused and then her own eyes narrowed in suspicion. "*Dumped* you? You wouldn't have reacted that way, even if you've never *been* dumped. Tell me the truth, Liv. What did that son of a—"

I interrupted her before she could piece it together. "He *dumped* me. That's what happened." I stood up.

"Liv…" she began.

"That's what happened, Mel. Just leave it alone. It's humiliating enough without having to give you a play by play." I said it more harshly than I meant to and when I caught the look on her face, I threw her an apologetic glance.

"Okay. Well, next time you get *dumped,* don't bother calling me for help." She threw the pillow she was holding to the floor.

"I'm sorry, Mel. I'm just not ready to talk about it. Okay?"

She studied me for a minute and nodded sadly. I walked down the carpeted stairs, feeling the plush white fibers between my toes. I looked down to see that I was barefoot. *Huh, when did that happen?* Brushing it off, I continued down the stairs thankful that her parents always slept in on Saturdays and wouldn't notice my retreat. My purse and shoes were in the front hallway by the door, so I slipped them on and left, making sure to quietly close the screen door so that it didn't slam shut.

As soon as I was outside, pure terror hit me like a wall. I felt so exposed that I nearly ran back inside. I forced myself to run home as quickly as I could, almost having a heart attack every time I saw someone. Before I knew it, I was running up my driveway, unaware of how I had even gotten there.

Quickly, I checked the time on my phone and breathed a sigh

of relief that my parents would be garage-saling so I could slip in unnoticed. I did a double-take of my phone, because surely the red ball indicating seventeen text messages couldn't be accurate. It was.

Every single one was from Chris.

My heart pounding wildly and my eyes darted from side to side as I walked up the steps to my front door, crossing it, slamming it, and locking it. I leaned back against the door and read through the texts.

9:31p.m. - Come back here.

9:34p.m. - Why did you take off like that?

9:42p.m. - We need to talk.

9:48p.m. - I'm coming to find you.

10:13p.m. - Why did you run away from me?

10:17p.m. - Come back and let's talk and put this misunderstanding behind us.

10:27p.m. - I love you.

10:51p.m. - Answer me now.

10:52p.m. - Forget it then, I knew you were just a child.

11:01p.m. - I'm sorry. I shouldn't have said that. Just come back over.

11:13p.m. - If you don't answer me soon it's over between us.

11:31p.m. - You have until midnight.

7:14a.m. - Good morning, beautiful. How did you sleep?

7:16a.m. - You never went home last night. Where are you?

7:42a.m. - We need to talk.

7:44a.m. - Stop ignoring me, Olivia.

7:45a.m. - Answer me now.

MY HANDS WERE SHAKING SO BADLY I could barely read the last few texts. I turned my phone off. How did he know that I hadn't gone home last night? Was he still watching my house?

The clock ticking in the kitchen sounded like hammer thuds with each second that passed. I kicked my shoes off and threw them in the closet. I didn't know what to do. I was exhausted but knew I'd never sleep with no one home to protect me. I was starving but couldn't stomach the thought of eating anything. I stood frozen in the kitchen with trembling hands as I stared at the clock.

Tick.

Tick.

Tick.

BRRRRRRRING! The sound of our old school rotary phone made me jump so high I nearly landed on the kitchen counter. My heart was racing, and my palms were so sweaty that I had to wipe them on my jeans. I stared at the phone while it rang, with no intention of answering it.

"Hello, you've reached the Jacksons. We are unavailable at the moment. Please leave a message and we will return your call at our earliest convenience." I always teased my mom about how stiff she sounded and the fact that no one used that kind of answering machine anymore, but I didn't feel the usual lightheartedness toward it I normally did. There was a long pause after the beep, and I expected the familiar click, meaning that the person on the other end of the line had decided not to leave a message. It didn't come. Instead, Chris's voice came through the machine and sent shivers of terror down my spine.

"Hello this is Chris. I'm looking for Olivia… Uh, there seems to be a problem with her phone. Please call me as soon as you get this."

The machine clicked off and left me standing there in deafening silence. I stood as motionless as a statue, holding my breath until I couldn't hold it anymore. *He's never going to leave me alone, is he? What the hell am I supposed to do?* My body began to tremble.

I let my breath out in a gush as I heard car doors slam and my parents' voices coming up the driveway through the open window. I rushed over to the answering machine and erased his message, and then ran straight down the stairs to my room, closing the door. I could hear my parents' excitement and knew they must have lucked into something good.

"Olivia?" my dad's voice rang out. I heard him talking to my mom. "She must be home, the door's locked now. Olivia?"

My throat felt so dry.

I wanted to tell him everything, but I knew I couldn't. They'd never let me out again, and who knows what my dad might decide to do to Chris. Amanda would tell them she warned me, and she'd be right. I should've listened to her. *Frig I wish that I had listened to her.* I swallowed a few times, opened the door a crack, and called out.

"Yeah, Dad, I'm here. I'm gonna get some more sleep." My voice sounded so hollow in my ears that I prayed he didn't notice.

"Sure, sure. Come up later, I wanna show you what we got!" He sounded as excited as a kid in a candy store.

I clicked my door shut again and let my breath out. When I moved to change my clothes, the room started spinning. I reached my hand out to steady myself against the wall and bent over with my other hand leaning on one knee. Once more, I breathed in and out slowly, trying to steady myself. Finally, I felt stable enough to tiptoe to my dresser to get some sweats.

In the bathroom, I avoided looking at myself in the mirror

and turned on the shower. My clothes went into the trash can, and I stepped under the scalding water. I needed it to be as hot as possible to clean off the memories of the previous night.

As I stood in the water, I knew it should hurt more than it did. I just couldn't feel it. The water dripped down my head and into my eyes as I stared at the drops sliding down the light-blue shower tiles. A rogue stream cascaded in a different direction than the rest of the beams of water. I wondered what was causing it to do that. Was it trying to escape? Go against the grain? Probably just dirt stuck underneath.

Eventually, the water started getting cold. I turned it off and stepped out onto the maroon floor mat. I still felt unclean. There was no towel in the bathroom, so I just put on my sweats while my hair dripped water all over the floor.

My parents were still talking excitedly, allowing me to tiptoe back across the hall to my room. In my bed, I pulled the covers right up to my eyes while my hair soaked through my pillow. I stared at my dark blue accent wall until my eyes blurred so badly that I couldn't make it out anymore. Then and only then did I close my eyes.

"Liv? Are you okay?" My mother was beside me.

I sat up slowly. "What? Yeah, I'm okay, Mom."

When had I fallen asleep? I rubbed my eyes and tried to focus on her face. She was sitting on the edge of my bed beside me, knitting her brows, and she leaned forward and put her wrist up against my forehead.

"Hmm, no fever."

I noticed that she was wearing her work clothes and I stared at her in confusion.

"Why are you wearing your work clothes on a Saturday?" I asked.

"It's Monday." She tilted her head with concern.

Monday? When did that happen? I racked my brain, trying to piece together the weekend—but it was blank.

"Monday? Are you sure?" It couldn't be Monday already. I

wasn't ready for the weekend to be over. I wasn't ready to face anyone.

"Yes, I think I'd know if it was Monday or not. You need to get up or you'll be late for school." She stood and patted my leg.

I moaned. "Can I stay home today? I don't feel well." I knew full well what her answer would be. I wanted to beg her to let me stay home, but she'd need a reason. I wanted to tell her how scared I was, but I didn't.

"No fever, no staying home. You know the rules, Liv." She walked to the door, stepping over half a dozen things on the floor.

"And maybe you can clean your room after school? For once?" She sighed and left.

I debated appealing to my dad but thought better of it. He was even more of a tyrant when it came to school. *No school, no future.* I sat on the edge of my bed and looked down at the clothes I had apparently been wearing for two days. I felt my heart begin to race at the thought of having to go to school, but what choice did I have? I couldn't tell my parents what had happened. This was my burden to bear. There was no one I could trust with this. I'd gotten myself into this mess, and I would need to get myself out.

I wanted Chris to leave me alone, and I was terrified that he wouldn't. My bed called to me, yet I couldn't just hide under the covers forever. Eventually, I'd have to get up and face this. I figured it might as well be now. I got up, showered, and threw some clothes on. And then I headed to school.

7

I walked through the parking lot of Gibbons, eyeing every car suspiciously. Out of the corner of my eye, I saw a black car crawling toward me and my heart leaped into my throat. I stood there frozen, holding my breath as it got closer to me and then slowly exhaled as it drove by and I realized it wasn't him. *It's not even a Camaro,* I scolded myself.

The school had an ominous feel to it despite the bright cream-colored bricks on the outside. I walked through the door, and something seemed off right away. Two girls walked by in their plaid school uniforms, holding their books to their chests, and stopped dead in their tracks as I walked toward them. I paused and looked around to see what they were staring at, but there was no one behind me. They burst into laughter as the one closest to me covered her mouth and began whispering to her friend.

Okay…that was weird. I pulled my backpack closer to myself and shook off the bad impression they'd left as I headed to my locker.

"There she is!" I heard someone whisper loudly and turned to see a finger pointed in my direction.

Again, I looked around to find I was the only person in the

vicinity. Insecurity rose in me like a bubble about to burst. *This can't be about you; you're just being paranoid.* I wanted to believe my own comforting words, but it felt like everyone was staring at me.

"I can't believe she showed. What a skank."

The words came from a girl I hardly knew as she walked by me in the hallway. She and her friend gave me a look with eyebrows raised, then faced forward and continued walking.

What the hell is happening right now? I asked myself nervously. It felt like I was in a really bad made-for-TV high school drama. My palms started to sweat as I quickened my pace to my locker. Every laugh seemed to be pointed in my direction. Every whisper, I thought, was about me. My friend Stacey stood by her locker, beside mine.

"Hey, Stacey," I said wearily.

She turned and had a look of surprise on her face. "I hear *you* had a good weekend," she said as she stifled a laugh. My eyebrows creased as a look of confusion and hurt came over my face.

"What's that supposed to mean?" I mumbled.

She snorted, closed her locker, and walked away without a word. I stood there in shock, watching her leave. Only then did I notice the folded sheet of lined paper sticking out of my locker. My heart was in my throat again as I reached for it. *Did Chris put this here*? My eyes darted back and forth so quickly that the row of lockers started to look blurry. *Chill out. He doesn't even know where your locker is.* My breath was coming out in shaky gasps as I grabbed the note and opened my locker to read it. I didn't want an audience for whatever this was.

SLUT!

The word was written in thick black capital letters. It was written in pen, so someone had taken a great deal of time to craft this. I stared, reading and re-reading it again and again.

Slut? Who would write this? Had someone seen what happened at Chris's apartment? I fought back the tears pricking behind my eyes and crumpled the paper in anger, tossing it to the back of my locker. In possession of my books, I slammed the door shut, catching the attention of a few students who were across the hall. I shoved the books in my bag and started toward homeroom. If I could just sink in my seat and pretend that everything was fine... *It's going to be fine,* I told myself over and over again.

"Hey, Liv!"

Bobby Reed stood in front of me. Class clown. On the football team. Average grades. My brain was processing things slowly in little snippets, as though that was all it was capable of at the moment. I looked up at his unnaturally blond shaggy hair as he ran his hand through it, probably in an attempt to smooth it over. It didn't work.

"Hey, Bobby," I said flatly.

"We should go out sometime."

His tone made my face flood with uncomfortable heat. He wrapped his arm around my shoulders, and I jerked away quickly. He laughed.

"Oh, come on. Don't be like that. I hear you're not such a prude anymore. You owe me a good time for shooting me down last year."

He had positioned himself directly in front of me, my back pressed against a locker. His arm hit the wall, cutting off my escape, and he leaned in far too close. My skin felt like it was on fire, and I wanted to bolt.

"Get away from me!" My voice was high and pitchy as I ducked under his arm and clutched my chest.

"There she goes again, already moving on to the next guy."

The voice came from across the hall, but when I looked to see who'd said it, I found five or six girls staring at me with their arms crossed. A few lockers down, Katie Bryan looked way too smug not to have had something to do with all of this. Wasn't she dating that guy Chris worked with? I glared at her as the hallway began to stretch on, getting narrower and narrower like in a horror movie. The blood whooshed inside my ears at a deafening volume.

Someone bumped into me and my bag fell to the ground.

"Sorry." The tone was sarcastic, and I knew that bumping into me was no accident. All I could hear was ringing inside my ears as I watched my bag float through the air, and felt myself getting pushed backward through a door.

"Liv."

It faintly sounded like someone was calling my name.

"Liv!"

It was getting louder but I still couldn't place it.

"LIV!"

Suddenly Mela was in my face, shouting at me. I shook my head and snapped out of the trance.

"Mela?" I asked softly.

"Are you okay?" She sounded panicked as she set my bag down.

"Huh?" I was trying to piece together where we were. Gray stalls, silver trash can, white sinks, light yellow painted walls, unforgiving fluorescent lights… The washroom. I looked at Mela and her mouth was moving, but no sound was coming out of it. I stared a little harder.

"Liv? Answer me!" She was gently shaking my shoulders.

"What?" *Pull it together, Liv.*

"I said, what really happened Friday night?" she asked gently.

Heat flooded my face instantly. "I don't want to talk about it," I mumbled.

"You really scared me, Liv. I've never seen you like that. I'm your best friend, you can trust me."

She stared at me, her face so worried I wanted to pull her into a hug and sob on her shoulder. I desperately wanted to tell her but at the same time I didn't. As long as no one knew what had really happened, I could pretend it never had. *If I say it out loud, it'll be real.* I hugged my arms around myself.

"He tried to—" I started and then stopped. She raised her eyebrows in surprise and waited for me to go on. I took a deep breath and continued. "He tried to force himself on me. He wouldn't stop even though I begged him to."

Her hand flew up to her mouth as she stifled a gasp.

Flashes of that night flew through my mind. My stifled scream, the sound of his belt undoing, the sensation of his hot breath on my face. I shivered, and my eyes filled with tears that threatened to spill over. I didn't bother wiping them away.

"Holy crap, Liv! How did you get away?" she asked with wide eyes.

"His roommate came in and I took off." I shrugged one shoulder as though it was no big deal. My shaking hands betrayed me, though.

"I'm so sorry, Liv," Mela whispered. She immediately pulled me into a hug, and I let my head rest on her shoulder as tears spilled down my cheeks and soaked her shirt.

"Everyone is talking about me," I whispered through my tears.

"They all think that you slept with him."

She spoke softly but it felt like a brick had dropped into my stomach. I stood there, putting all the pieces together in my mind. The note, the whispers, the laughs, Bobby Reed…

"Why would they think that?" I pulled away and wiped my tears on my sleeve. My hands were shaking, and Mela was so blurry I could hardly focus on her.

"Katie Bryan spread it around. I guess Chris bragged about it to her boyfriend, and she spent the weekend texting everyone about it." She grimaced.

Suddenly my emotions changed from terrified to furious.

At that moment, I hated Katie with every fiber of my being. We'd known each other since kindergarten, and though we'd never officially been friends, I didn't think we were enemies. Until now. I was burning with anger and my fists kept clenching and unclenching.

Her ears must have been burning because the door opened and there she was. Katie looked me up and down and smiled sweetly.

"Guess you're not such a saint after all, Olivia. The Virgin Mary deflowered at last. It's about time someone took you down a peg," she said.

Mela gasped and placed herself before me.

I saw red. Flashes of Chris holding me down, me running in socked feet, students snickering, thinking I had given myself to that monster—all because she'd told them I had. Before I knew what I was doing, I had sidestepped Mela, my left arm moved back, and my dad's words were in my ears.

"Keep your thumb outside your fist when you're punching, or you'll break it."

He had been talking me through self defense, but this was close enough.

I tucked my thumb in front of the first and second knuckles and punched Katie Bryan right across the right side of her jaw. As soon as my fist connected with her face, I regretted my decision. She was on the ground, holding her jaw and wailing something about ending me socially.

"Liv!" Mela screamed in shock.

Holy crap, I just punched someone in the face. My left hand was throbbing, and my face was so hot I was sure it was melting off. I wished more than anything that I could take that moment back, but it was too late. I looked at Mela in desperation.

"Go!" she cried, and pointed to the door.

She was right, I needed to get out of there. I scooped up my bag and flew out the door without looking back. I stood there for a second debating between emptying my locker or just fleeing school property and decided I didn't have time for pit stops.

As fast as I could, I headed toward the exit. In my head, the film of my fist connecting with her jaw played over and over again. *Oh my gosh, what did I just do? I'm dead. I'm so dead.* I continued walking and avoided eye contact with everyone, hoping that I could just silently leave without calling attention.

But more snickers reached my ears as I passed by packs of students. *Thank God no one got that on video.* It seemed to take me forever to get through the crowd. Had there always been so many students here? Or was this the universe's way of making sure I paid for what I'd done? Finally, the door materialized about twenty feet away. *Yes!*

"Ms. Jackson!" The loud call came from behind me.

No! I froze in place. *Crap, crap, crap! Maybe I can still make it.* I took a step forward.

"Don't you dare!" It was Mr. Koffra. Students littered the hallway, a sea of plaid uniforms watching the scene with mouths wide open in shock. I slowly turned and saw Katie standing beside him triumphantly, holding her now tear-stained face. *Crap.*

"You're wanted in the principal's office. Immediately."

He gestured in the opposite direction I had taken. I thought about ignoring him and just walking out, but I didn't want to get expelled. I didn't want to jeopardize my position on the track team, especially now. With a sigh of defeat, I walked slowly past Mr. Koffra, who was consoling Katie. A bruise was already forming on the side of her face, and I cringed as I replayed the blow in my head once more. It felt like a rock was now lodged in the pit of my stomach. *I can't believe I did this.*

When I got to the office, Ms. Goodwin, the principal, motioned me over while the secretary looked at me with what appeared to be a mix of pity and disgust. As soon as I walked into her office, she closed the door behind me—never a good sign. I sat down on the chair across from her desk. It was so full of files and papers that I could barely see her as she took her place behind it.

"You hit Katie Bryan?" she didn't waste any time.

My eyes filled with tears as I nodded.

"That's inexcusable, Olivia," she said quietly.

I squirmed in my seat uncomfortably. *Of course it was inexcusable. People don't just punch other people in the face.* I felt like I was losing it. I stared down at my lap focusing on the slight rip in my jeans. Ms. Goodwin's sigh was heavy.

"What happened?" she asked stiffly.

I don't know what happened! I wanted to scream at her; instead, I stayed quiet. Maybe if I just said nothing, she'd let me leave.

"You've got to give me something here, Olivia." Her soft tones were just making this worse. I wanted to be swallowed up and forgotten about.

"I don't know what came over me." My voice cracked on the last word. I looked up at her, finally, and noticed the new wrinkles around her eyes. Her dark hair was dry and starting to turn gray and the bags under her eyes were large enough to magnify the toll this place was taking on her.

"This isn't the first time you've lost control like this."

My eyes flashed angrily toward her, but the pity in her expression made me want to scream.

"I know," I said.

That time had been different, though. It was unfair of her to even bring that up. I had been slammed up against a locker by a girl three grades older than me because she thought I was flirting with her boyfriend. *Was I supposed to just sit there and take it?* No one had my back; I had to take care of myself.

"Your grades are good, and I know you're an excellent athlete—but you've been showing up late, giving your teachers attitude, not turning in your homework on time. What's going on with you?"

A surge of feelings threatened to come up to the surface as a reaction to her kindness, but I shoved it down.

"I'm fine," I said quietly.

She had always been kind to me, but what good would confiding in her do? What if she didn't believe me? What if she told my parents?

"You're not fine, Olivia. Something is clearly wrong."

She waited for me to answer; I sat there in silence. It was an uncomfortable standoff. She was right, something was definitely wrong, but I couldn't tell her. I waited for the suspension that was no doubt on its way. I had never been suspended before, and my parents were going to be so disappointed.

"You've left me no choice here." She sighed again. "Punching a student in the face goes far beyond anything we can tolerate here. I can't look the other way this time, Olivia."

The rock in my stomach was growing. This sounded more serious than a suspension. Suddenly I was praying for something that had terrified me a minute ago.

"You are expelled from Gibbons High," she said with finality.

I stiffened, completely immobile, as though perhaps she might change her mind and I could just go back in time. No such luck.

"Did you hear what I said?" she asked.

No sound came out of my mouth when I opened it. Expelled? I mean I knew that hitting someone was bad but, expelled?

"Please don't do this, Ms. Goodwin. Coach Stewart just told me that I might have a spot on the Lion's Track Team in the spring. If you expel me, I'll lose that chance." I hated begging, but I needed her to change her mind.

"I'm sorry about that." She sounded less sorry and more final than before, though. "You probably should have considered that before assaulting a fellow student."

Assault? I flinched at the word. "Is there anything I can do to change your mind?"

"I'm afraid not."

Slowly, I nodded and stood up as I hitched my bag onto my shoulder. I couldn't help but wonder if my skin tone had anything to do with this decision. The thought was fleeting, but it was there, nonetheless. I was a model student and a competitive athlete. All Katie Bryan had ever contributed to that school were long legs and a low IQ. *Unfair, unfair, unfair.*

"I hope you'll begin to make better choices, Olivia. You really could have a bright future ahead of you, and I'd hate to see you throw that away."

My eyebrows rose automatically. "Well, I guess my future isn't your concern anymore, Ms. Goodwin," I said tersely.

No school, no future.

I turned and opened her door. Shoving down the fear and sadness, I stared at the ground as I left the office. Mela came toward me, but the look on my face stopped her dead in her tracks. I shook my head as I turned my back on everyone and quickly walked out on the future I no longer had.

8

The multicolored living room couch was my haven for the moment. The minutes passed by and my parents said nothing. I stole a glance at my dad and cringed at the look of disappointment on his face, and the way he kept opening his mouth to say something and slamming it shut in exasperation.

If only I could crawl onto his lap like I had when I was a kid… I resisted the urge. Instead, I feigned interest in the stain on his orange t-shirt while avoiding eye contact. I heard my mom sigh; again. I gripped the couch cushions tightly, trying to breathe through the pain that was growing in the middle of my chest.

I had no idea what Ms. Goodwin had said to them, but my imagination was running wild. All I knew was that she had called each of them, and they had left work early to meet me at home.

"Olivia. Tell us what happened." My mom's voice was gentle, but I still flinched at the sound.

"We already know the whole story, so don't bother trying to leave anything out," my dad chimed in. His words filled me with dread.

There goes trying to lie my way out of this. I took a deep breath to calm my racing heart and wiped my palms onto my pants; again. How long had we been sitting here for? It felt like hours. The clock told me that it had only been a few minutes. Another deep breath, and I blurted out the words.

"I punched a bully in the face." It was all I could think to say that might make it seem less awful.

"A bully? Was she hurting you?" my mom piped up quickly.

I paused while I tried to think of what to say next. "Not…physically."

They sighed again. I stared out the window at the dark clouds forming. The wind was swaying the trees back and forth, and the rain began pelting the windows.

"Olivia, you can't just punch people in the face! What's going on with you?" my dad demanded.

I shrank back at the sound of his booming voice and tried to melt into the couch. He was right, normal people didn't just physically assault others, not even a Katie Bryan.

"Nothing's going on with me. I'm fine." *You wouldn't understand,* I added to myself.

"You're clearly not fine. You've been moody and distant for months. Is this about that boy you're dating? Did you two break up?" My mom sounded sympathetic and soft, but the mention of Chris sent a shot of fear through me.

I stiffened. I couldn't tell them what he'd done. They had enough worries of their own.

"It's not about him. I'm fine." I tried to sound convincing. This was my burden to bear, not theirs.

"We used to be so close, Liv. Talk to me." Her pleading nearly broke through my shell, but not quite.

"I'm fine, Mom, really."

I had said the word *fine* so many times that it was starting to sound weird to me. *Fine, fine, fine.* I wasn't even sure how to spell it anymore. My dad shot me an incredulous look. I clearly wasn't fooling him. He had always had this way of knowing when I was lying.

"You know what this means, don't you? You'll have to go to the 'alternative' school now." His use of air quotes was almost laughable, but I wasn't in the mood to smile.

I sank back in defeat. The pain in my chest was flaring up so badly that I wanted to reach in and tear out whatever was causing it. Instead, I sat there motionless, waiting for the conversation to end. The truth was, I didn't want to go to a new school. The thought of losing my friends and having to start over made me want to cry, or scream, or hit something. Maybe all three.

"Do you honestly have nothing to say for yourself?" I had never heard my dad sound so angry.

You are the good one, he had always told me. I was the one he didn't have to worry about. I flinched at his volume and jumped as a peal of thunder boomed in the distance. My mom turned to him and put one hand on his leg.

"Honey, maybe we should all calm down and reconvene at a later time."

Quickly, I nodded in agreement. I had no intention of reconvening at any point, though. As soon as I was free, I planned to pack some of my things and take off. I could stay at Mela's for a while.

"Can I go now?" I asked quietly as I stared at the carpet.

"You may."

I stood up, avoided eye contact as I walked by my parents, and went down the stairs to my room. I closed the door behind me and leaned back against it for a moment, gathering strength to pack.

My shoulders slumped forward in defeat as I pushed off the door and walked over to my closet. How could everything have changed so fast in less than a week? I began stuffing clothes into an old duffel bag.

CRACK! Another flash of lightning crossed the black sky, and the thunder that followed shook my entire house. Was I really going to go out in that? I dropped the bag on the floor, quietly cracked opened my door, and pressed my ear to the gap.

"...can't believe that she would do this," my dad whispered angrily.

"She must have had a reason though. It's not like Olivia to just hit someone." My mom's voice was calming. I could practically see her rubbing my dad's arm the way she had done a thousand times. She was usually soothing him about my sister, not about me.

"Well, she's grounded...for a long time. We should've paid more attention to who she was going out with. She's changed so much. I barely recognize her anymore." His voice broke on the last word. I swallowed hard as tears filled my eyes.

"Honey, I really don't think that grounding her is going to solve anything. Maybe a fresh start will be good for her. I've been so worried—"

I closed the door before I could hear any more. I held my breath as the door clicked shut and then let it out again when I heard their voices still up in the living room.

Sitting on the edge of my bed, I leaned down with my head in my hands. What was I going to do? I couldn't just leave. Chris was still out there, and I didn't know what he would do to me if I ran into him. I shivered at the thought. Besides, my parents had been through enough, and running away would only make everything worse.

The trees blew violently in the wind, back and forth. I lay down on top of my covers and put on my headphones to drown out the world; it didn't work. Yet another bright flash of lightning lit up my room, but I was tired of flinching. I turned up the music.

The view of my white stucco ceiling made me remember lying in the same position as a child. At least then my problems were about skipping ropes and skinned knees. Now it felt like I had been thrown into a world I wasn't ready for. The train was leaving the station, and I was standing on the tracks.

I turned off the music and pulled out a journal to try to clear my head, but the pen just hovered above the paper lacking direction. I sat there staring at the blank page, willing myself to come up with a brilliant idea that would get me out of this funk.

Another peal of thunder shook the house. Finally, I accepted that the storm was bound to rule the night, and I lay in bed for hours, listening to the wind howl and the drops tap against my window.

At some point, my parents headed up the stairs to bed without saying goodnight. They probably thought I was already asleep. As much as I wanted sleep to come, it felt like it never would. I continued staring out the window until my eyes eventually closed, and dreams of simpler times danced through my head. Things might look different soon. At least I hoped so; because for now, they looked very, very bleak.

9

Get over here ASAP, we need to get ready for the beach party tonight!

I glanced at the text from Mela as I grabbed my headphones and threw on my shoes. *Do I really want to go to a party tonight?* I pondered the question as I filled up my water bottle at the kitchen sink. The word NOVEMBER stared at me in block letters from the calendar on the wall.

Don't you dare bail on me. It's been weeks since we hung out. You are NOT getting out of this one!

I snorted. Trust Mela to know I was thinking of bailing on her. The truth was I had bailed on her every time she had asked to hang out lately. I just hadn't been ready to go anywhere or see anyone; not even Mela.

I tightened the lid on my bottle as I walked out the door and headed to the beach for my run. My stomach shrank a little as I left the shelter of my home and stepped outside. *He doesn't care about you anymore, Liv, it's been weeks.* I repeated the words over and over as I felt calm spread through me. Chris wasn't lurking behind every bush in my mind anymore. Six weeks was a long time not to hear from someone.

I had spent most of it holed up in the safety of my room, journaling, thinking, staring at the wall, and binge-watching old shows, but the last week or so I'd been venturing out more and more in preparation of my impending return to the world of education.

I took off at a steady pace down the street and quickly reached the sand. I never grew tired of the water or the way the sun sparkled on it, and I breathed a sigh of relief as soon as it was in sight. I set a steady pace and let the rhythm of my steps and the music in my ears carry me away. The beach was pretty well deserted as the tourists had left weeks earlier, and it wasn't close enough to Thanksgiving for new arrivals. I liked it better this way.

A group of seagulls looking for scraps took flight in sync as I ran by them. I watched them fly away together over the water. They all looked the same, like a family. I felt the familiar pang of longing to know who I belonged to. *Jealous of a flock of seagulls, Liv? Really?*

My steady running pace had turned to a sprint as I had let my mind wander, so I slowed down to a light jog to catch my breath and turned around to start heading back. I needed to get ready for the beach party before Mela had a conniption fit.

Eyes on the water and my mind all over the place, I didn't notice the jogger coming from the other direction until it was too late. I slammed into him so hard that my earbuds fell out and I spun around, landing with a thud in the sand. I was completely disoriented as I tried to get my bearings. My heart thudded quickly in my chest. *Was it Chris?* The sun was blinding as I looked up. Then, like an eclipse, a guy I had never seen blocked the light and stretched out his hand, offering to help me up.

"Are you okay?" His voice was full of concern.

There was a whole lot of beach, and yet we managed to smash into each other. But at least he wasn't Chris. He was tall, with dirty blond hair and an athletic body. I put my hand in his and let him pull me up. As our eyes connected, I saw that his were a mix of hazel and green with a yellow ring around the center. They were mesmerizing, and I felt my face flush as I realized I was still holding his hand and was now staring deeply into his eyes.

He was, in a word, gorgeous.

I quickly dropped his hand and stepped back.

"I'm sorry," we said at the same time. He smiled; I couldn't help but stare.

"I'm Lucas," he said pleasantly.

"I'm Olivia," I replied in shy mode. "I'm sorry I slammed into you." I was so embarrassed.

He laughed, and the sound immediately put me at ease. "You can run into me anytime, Olivia."

"Liv," I replied. "My friends call me Liv."

He nodded as though this was crucial information and glanced at his watch with what looked like regret. I did the same and was startled to see that I was now late.

"I've gotta go," he said. There was definite regret in his tone. "You sure you're okay?"

"Yeah, yeah I'm fine. I've gotta get going too," I said quickly. I was trying to play it somewhat cool after such a mortifying introduction. I turned to leave, and he touched my arm lightly. I turned with surprise.

"Seriously? You're not even going to give me your number?" he cried putting his hand to his heart in mock dismay.

It was my turn to laugh. "You never asked for it." I shrugged as I put my earphones back in my ears and jogged away quickly in the opposite direction, leaving him staring after me.

I got home in record time and quickly sent Mela a text.

Sorry, I'll be over in 10.

I took the fastest shower in the history of my life, grabbed several outfit choices, all of my makeup, and headed up the stairs.

"Where are you off to in such a hurry?" My mom's voice behind me made me jump.

"I'm sleeping at Mela's tonight, remember?" I said quickly as I stepped toward the door.

"Oh, that's still happening?"

I cringed at the sound of surprise in her voice. I guess I *had* basically been a recluse for the last few weeks.

"Yeah. I mean, I figure with school starting on Monday, I should probably get back out to the land of the living." I tried to sound more upbeat than I felt.

"Might be a good idea," she said softly. "Take the K car," she added.

I made a face. The K car was an old, rust-colored Dodge Aries. My parents had shocked me by giving it to me when my mom upgraded her car. It was hideous, but it beat the bus any day.

I stepped outside and considered just walking, but I was super late so I jumped in and started it, took a deep breath, and threw it into reverse, hitting the gas as fast as I could while a distinct beeping—like one would normally hear coming out of a large truck—began. I put the car into drive as soon as I was able to, and the beeping stopped.

No one around seemed to have paid special notice to the sound, and I drove away, silently cursing my dad yet again for finding that stupid back-up beeper at a yard sale. Whenever I took the car out, I tried to make sure that I was always parked in a pull-through spot, no matter how far away it was. Thankfully Mela lived about a two-minute drive from my place, and I was there before she could text me for the third time, asking if I was on my way yet.

Avoiding their perfectly landscaped lawn and gardens, I walked up her front steps and through the door without knocking. Almost two decades of friendship had allowed me some privileges. I climbed the stairs and pushed open Mela's bedroom door to find her sitting at the mirror, putting the final touches on her makeup.

I hadn't been here since the night of the attack. I hesitated in the doorway and then forced myself to step through and put it out of my mind. She looked at me through the mirror of her makeup table and sighed as she assessed my state.

"Liv the Unready," she said.

"I'm sorry, I lost track of time on my run. I'll leave my hair curly and skip the makeup?" I offered. I knew she wouldn't take me up on it.

"Just hurry up, I want to get there," she said excitedly.

I didn't dawdle and settled on jean capris and a green tank top with a three-quarter length, white zip-up sweater. I straightened my hair, did my makeup, and was ready in under twenty minutes.

Mela looked much more daring in a black mini skirt and bright red crop top, but she could rock it. We looked at each other and nodded in approval. I had been so busy getting ready that I hadn't even told her about meeting the guy on the beach. Now that I thought about it, I wasn't even sure it merited an announcement. I'd met him for two seconds, and I hadn't even given him my number. Not exactly breaking news.

"Let's go!" Mela's voice broke through my thoughts.

"Okay."

Suddenly, I became enthusiastic about my last beach party before starting at a new school. Who knew what would happen there? I decided that I would let loose a little and get lost in the atmosphere for once. I hadn't really seen anyone in weeks, and I needed to get back to living my life. Armed with a couple of wine coolers and no chaperones, we headed to the beach giggling with anticipation like the schoolgirls we were. I didn't know why, but I had a feeling it was going to be a good night.

10

Mela and I walked to the beach together, drinking wine coolers with linked arms and a carefree attitude. We'd been making this trek regularly for so long that I was surprised there weren't grooves in the pavement from our footprints. I gave Mela a sideways glance and swelled with gratitude for our friendship. No one had ever stuck around the way she had. The sun was setting over the water as we reached the sand.

"Oooh! Let's go to the rocks," I proposed.

The rocks by the lighthouse had always been my favorite spot, and when the sun was setting the view was spectacular. Mela looked at me with glassy eyes and burst into laughter. I stared at her with my eyebrows creased in confusion until I replayed in my mind how excited I had just gotten about rocks. I snorted. Clearly, the alcohol was kicking in.

"Come find Nate with me," she pleaded.

I noticed her stumble a little and figured it wouldn't be a bad idea to make sure she was with her boyfriend before I took off to watch the sunset. I grabbed her arm and we strolled on the beach side by side. Someone had driven a truck up onto the sand and was playing music loudly from a massive sound system. I saw a bonfire in the distance and pointed it out to Mela; we stumbled along together, giggling as we walked. I breathed in the salty sea air and enjoyed the feel of the wind through my hair. It made me feel so free and unburdened for the first time in a long time. Somewhere deep down I knew that alcohol was making me feel this way, and that wasn't right; but it was working tonight, so I decided to just enjoy the ride.

As we got closer to the fire, I caught sight of Nate and some of his friends. He was standing around with an easy smile on his face talking animatedly about something. Probably football since it was really the only time you couldn't shut him up. The rest of the time he was simply quiet and chill, always in a hoodie and eating some kind of candy. I smiled to myself when I saw the bag of licorice in his hand. We were getting closer now and my heart flew into my throat when I saw that the guy standing right next to him was Lucas. I swore under my breath.

"Liv?" Mela was staring at me as I turned my back to the fire, frantically looking for an exit point.

I didn't know what was wrong with me, but I knew I had to get out of there. I scolded myself for drinking because it was the worst possible time for me to be around someone like Lucas; I was way too uninhibited, and I didn't trust myself.

"I think I saw my sister back there!" My voice was high. I hoped that she didn't hear the fear in it.

"Really? I didn't see anyone…" Mela replied dubiously.

"I'm sure I did. I'll just go check! Meet you by the fire?" I didn't give her a chance to answer as I turned and practically ran in the opposite direction.

My sister and I weren't exactly close, so I could understand Mela's confusion. Running off to find her would be extremely uncharacteristic of me, but I couldn't think of another excuse, and I had to clear my head.

I headed for the rocks, breathing a sigh of relief that Lucas hadn't seen me. I carefully made my way to the farthest point, only stumbling two or three times, and plunked myself down to watch the rest of the sunset. The music drifted to me, but I couldn't quite make out the song; something with a lot of bass anyway. My head was definitely clearer since instant panic was an excellent buzz kill.

After a couple of minutes, I heard someone approaching and turned, expecting to find Mela. Instead, I was staring up at Lucas. Again.

"Hey," he said pleasantly.

"Hey," I replied warily.

He seemed to pick up on my mood.

"Do you want to be alone?" He turned slightly, as if to leave.

"No!" I blurted out way too loudly before I could gather my thoughts.

"Okay…"

He hesitated a little before sitting down beside me. *He must think I'm certifiable.*

"So. You know Nate." It came out as a statement instead of a question.

As soon as the words were out of my mouth, I realized that he would now know I'd seen him at the fire and taken off. I flushed with embarrassment, but to my surprise, he didn't bring it up and simply said, "Yeah, we go way back."

I nodded, afraid to say anything stupid again. We sat in silence for a while as the setting sun streaked the sky with yellow, pink, and purple clouds. It was absolutely breathtaking. And the silence between us wasn't an awkward one, I thought, so I let myself enjoy his company. I glanced over at him at the same time that he looked at me, and a spark of electricity shot through me. I quickly looked away and tried to control my breathing. I swore I'd never let myself develop feelings for another guy after Chris, what was I doing?

"How do you know Nate?" he asked.

"He's dating my best friend."

"Oh, cool. Mela, right?"

"You know her?" I tilted my head in confusion.

"Yeah, I've met her a few times."

"Huh. Weird. She's never mentioned you before."

He looked relieved at my words for some reason. "Maybe I didn't leave an impression."

My eyebrows raised automatically and without thinking, I replied. "That's not very likely." Heat instantly flooded my face as I waited for him to comment, but he let it pass.

"I think she's told me about you before," he said quietly after a moment.

"Oh yeah? What did she say?" I held my breath nervously.

"I could tell you, but then I'd have to kill you."

"Uh-huh." I gave him a half-smirk.

"Sorry, that was dumb." He grimaced.

"I mean…a little."

We laughed.

"Nate's like a brother to me," he explained. "I spend most of my time at his place so Mela and I have run into each other a few times."

"Really?" I was surprised.

Mela spent at least half her time at Nate's, so why had I never heard of Lucas before? She had some serious explaining to do. I made a mental note to grill her as soon as we were alone.

"Yeah, between football and Nate's place, I barely have to spend any time at my house at all," he added cheerfully.

Behind the smile, there was something I couldn't put my finger on. He had a reason not to spend much time at home, but I didn't want to make him uncomfortable, so I didn't ask.

"Let's go for a walk." He stood up quickly and put his hand out for me to grab. I looked at it hesitantly while he rolled his eyes and said, "It's *just* a walk."

Sure, I thought to myself, *just a walk. Ten minutes from now I'll be completely in love with you, but it's just a walk.* I sighed as I grabbed his hand and once more let him pull me up. I stumbled a little on the rocks, so he held my hand as I followed him to help steady me. I let go as soon as we were off the rocks.

He put his hands in his pockets and gave me the space I'm

sure he thought I wanted, but the truth was I didn't know what I wanted. We walked side by side down the beach for a while until we got to a stretch of sand lit up by the bonfire but still secluded enough to talk privately.

"This okay?" he asked quietly.

I nodded. We sat down on the white sand, side by side, with the tiniest bit of space between us. I was acutely aware of how close he was to me.

"So, Olivia, or Liv to your friends. Do you have a last name?"

Something about him made me want to lean closer just to hear him speak, but I sat still.

"Jackson?" I said it as though I had forgotten my last name. "Liv Jackson." I nodded more confidently the second time.

"Lucas O'Connell. But some of my friends call me Luke," he teased. I laughed out loud. He was so easy to be with.

"Lucas/Luke… I like it."

He smiled, and my heart skipped a beat. I looked away quickly. *Get a grip, Liv,* I scolded myself.

"What's your story?" he asked casually.

"That's a loaded question," I replied with a rueful smile.

For a second, his eyes scoured my face. "I didn't think so until just now."

"I don't have much of a story. I was born in Destin, adopted at three months old, and I've lived here in Fort Lauderdale ever since." I shrugged.

Now he stared at me with such intensity that I felt my stomach flip.

"I don't buy it."

"Don't buy what?" I asked.

"There's more to you than you let on." He seemed perceptive for a high school boy. He continued. "I'm sorry, I feel like I know you."

I blushed and laughed nervously. Not even ten minutes, he was good!

"So, what's *your* story?" I asked to change the subject.

He gave me a knowing smile and answered. "Well, I've always lived here. I live with my mom and my little brother, and I have an older brother who lives downtown. I play football and enjoy meeting pretty girls while running on the beach."

His smile was playful, but it made me grimace a little. *I guess I shouldn't be surprised that he meets girls while running,* I thought. He caught the look on my face and backtracked a little.

"Not that I'm in the habit of meeting random girls on the beach or anything."

I rolled my eyes. "Suuuure," I replied jokingly.

I smoothed my face into a smile so that he wouldn't realize the thought bothered me. Did it bother me? I wasn't sure. I mean, I barely knew him. I wanted to know if he had a girlfriend though, and that made me nervous. I couldn't bring myself to ask.

We sat and talked for a long time. He told me about his love of football, we joked about racing each other to see who was faster, and we both agreed that Nate and Mela were an odd match but seemed really happy. He told me about his two brothers and how he didn't spend much time with them. He never mentioned his dad, and I didn't ask; it seemed complicated.

I told him about my siblings and how they had all moved out years before, leaving me on my own. My brothers were out west, and my sister was planning on joining them as soon as she could.

"Are you going to run off to the West Coast too?" he teased.

"No," I said with finality. The way I said it made him pause and look over at me. I felt I owed him an explanation after that. "I'm sure it's beautiful and all, but people seem to leave here for there and never look back. I don't want to do that, I guess." I held my breath until the urge to cry passed.

Lucas simply nodded; he didn't push or pry, and I liked that. He told me ridiculous stories of how he and his brothers used to put a bucket of water in the freezer until it was almost frozen and then sneak into the bathroom when one of them was taking a shower to throw the entire bucket of ice water onto the unsuspecting victim. He had me laughing so hard my stomach hurt. I confided in him about my backup beeper and how humiliating it was to drive my car.

"Why don't you just disable it?" he asked through his laughter.

"How am I supposed to know how to do that?" I demanded.

He laughed even harder. I liked the sound. It was the kind of laugh that made you smile right along with it, as though you couldn't help yourself.

Mela was shrieking with laughter near the fire, which meant that she had found some more booze. I sighed. Lucas looked over at Mela and seemed to understand.

"You take care of her, don't you?" he asked softly.

"Yeah." I sighed again. "She doesn't always make the best decisions, and I worry about her," I confessed.

"What are you, like thirty-five?" he said with a smile.

I elbowed him in the ribs. "I'm just loyal. If I consider someone a friend, then I'll stand by them. Even when they're being a total douche."

He snorted and gave a small chuckle. "Good to know," he said as he winked at me. My heart skipped a beat as I checked the time on my phone.

"Shoot! We need to go." It was almost midnight. *How did that even happen?* It had only felt like a few minutes had passed.

Exhaling softly, he stood up, and pulled me to my feet. Third time. As we stood there facing each other, I realized how safe I felt with him. I didn't think I'd ever feel safe with the opposite sex again—but there I was, wondering if he might kiss me and kind of hoping he would. He stepped a little closer and seemed to wrestle with himself.

"Can I give you a hug goodbye?" he asked.

I smiled and nodded. He stepped toward me and my heart pounded in my chest. He gently wrapped his arms around my shoulders, and I pressed my head against his chest and hugged his waist. The corners of his mouth lifted into a small smile.

Just then Mela came barreling toward us at full speed, with Nate and her friend Steph dragging behind her. I jumped away from Lucas like we had been caught in bed together.

"Where have you *been*?" Mela screamed at me.

My face grew hot instantly as her eyes went back and forth between Lucas and me with her eyebrows raised high.

"Umm," I stammered.

She stood there staring at me waiting for an explanation while the silence grew to uncomfortable proportions. Finally, Nate came to the rescue.

"Hey, I see you two have finally met," he said with his usual easy smile. He had always been great at easing any tension.

I sent a *we're-going-to-talk-about-this-later* look toward Mela.

"We're late. We gotta go, like, now." She grabbed my free hand and started pulling me away from Lucas. I looked at him apologetically as Mela dragged me away.

"I'll see you later?" I mumbled pathetically.

"When?" he demanded with amusement in his eyes.

Mela kept dragging Steph and me up the beach. He knew I was intentionally not giving him my number. I shrugged with a smirk as I jogged backward, and he shook his head in disbelief.

"I'll find you!" he promised.

Giggling, I turned to run back to Mela's house.

"Who *was* that?" Steph demanded as we ran breathlessly through the street.

"Trouble," I answered with a laugh; and I knew without a doubt that he was the good kind of trouble.

11

The walk home seemed much longer than usual, probably due to our third wheel. Steph Grayson was nice, but I didn't love sharing my best friend with her. She had bright purple hair that she'd likely change next week, pale blue eyes, and was as thin as a rail.

Mela was pretty good at limiting the overlap of our time together, so it didn't bother me too much when she crashed our hangouts. I figured she was going to sleep at Mela's with us because her parents were even stricter than mine, and judging by the glassy look in her eyes, she was in no condition to make an appearance at home.

The night was quiet as we walked down the middle of the street. The only lights came from the moon and the spaced-out streetlamps. It was peaceful and still, the way I liked it.

As soon as the three of us snuck into Mela's house and were up in her bedroom, I turned to her and simply said, "Spill."

She knew Lucas and had never mentioned him. That was top of the weird scale for Mela since she had tried to hook me up with literally every other friend of whatever guy she happened to be dating. Steph looked confused, but Mela looked down at the ground while her face grew a deep shade of crimson.

"Okay, okay: Lucas O'Connell." She said it like an announcement. "He's Nate's best friend. They've known each other forever, and he's a really nice guy."

My eyes narrowed. "That's it? What aren't you telling me?"

I knew there had to be a reason she had never brought him up before. Having her best friend date her boyfriend's best friend would be too tempting for her to ignore, especially if it might potentially have gotten me away from Chris.

"His home life is...complicated." She threw a quick sideways glance to Steph, who was listening intently.

I understood her meaning. Steph was quite the gossip. Evidently, this was something of a sensitive nature, so I would have to wait until Steph was asleep to get the rest of Lucas's story. I sighed in frustration and then feigned starvation a few minutes later as I excused myself to go down to the kitchen. I had spent so many years in this part of Mela's house that it felt like my second home. It was small, with green cabinets and linoleum floors. It was hideous, and I loved it.

I waited at the small kitchen table, and it wasn't long before I heard Mela tiptoeing down the hall toward me. The sheepish look on her face made me snort out loud. She grabbed a glass of water and quietly joined me at the table.

"Steph passed out." She rolled her eyes as she said it. I didn't much care what Steph did at this point. My curiosity was burning me up.

"I'm not sure how much I'm allowed to say," she continued. "Nate swore me to secrecy when it happened."

"When *what* happened?" My eyes grew wide.

She looked so uncomfortable that I almost didn't want to force her to tell me, but I needed to know now. If he was some kind of psycho, then that was crucial information. I'd had enough nasty surprises lately to last me a lifetime. I sat quietly at the table and waited for her to go on.

"A while ago, Nate asked me to go pick Lucas up because he was at work and couldn't leave. This was during your hiatus from socialization, or I would've asked you to come with me. Lucas doesn't live in the greatest neighborhood, so I wanted to get out of there fast, ya know?"

I nodded but could feel the hairs on my arm rising. Something wasn't right with the situation but as if it were a car wreck on the highway, I couldn't look away.

"I pulled up to his house and it looked rough on the outside," she went on. "The paint was super faded and chipped, there was a rusted out, junky car in the driveway, and I could hear screaming from inside the house. I didn't know what to do, Liv." Her eyes welled up with tears, and I could feel that my face had frozen into a composed look so that she wouldn't see the fear in my eyes.

"What happened?" I whispered.

"No one was coming out, so I went up to the house. I could hear a man screaming at a woman and her shouting back at him. I don't know what they were yelling about but it sounded really heated. Then I heard Lucas shout *NO*, and the woman was screaming and screaming."

I put my hand up to stop her. I didn't know how much more I could handle. Her head was in her hands though, and she didn't see me.

"The man stormed out of the house and practically shoved me off the step. He was gross, Liv. Beer belly hanging out of his tiny shirt, stains, greasy hair, you know the type." She shuddered. "The woman was crying hysterically inside, and the man drove off in the piece-of-crap car. All of a sudden, Lucas was at the door with a backpack, and a bruise starting to form on the side of his face. He just smiled, Liv, like nothing was wrong! He asked if I was ready to go and that was that. I think he's been mostly staying at Nate's ever since."

My heart was so heavy, it felt like someone had dropped a hundred-pound weight on it.

"Anything else?" I asked warily.

"No. I tried to talk to Nate about it, but he got all weird and shrugged it off like it was no big deal. I could still tell it was. He told me not to tell anyone," she confessed.

"Who was the woman?"

"I think it was his mom."

I felt my eyes fill with tears and looked away quickly. All I wanted to do in that moment was find Lucas and throw my arms around him. He had been so casual about his home life, making it sound as if he just liked to be at Nate's when in reality, he was getting beaten up protecting his mom. No wonder I felt so safe with him. I looked back over at Mela, and she was snoring into her arm on the table; she was such a lightweight.

Gently I woke her up and got her into her bed. I lay down on the air mattress she had set up for me earlier and pulled the blanket over my head. I tried to fall asleep but couldn't, so I just stared into the darkness.

I stayed awake the entire night, with thoughts constantly circling my head. *Should I say something to Lucas?* He'd be embarrassed if I did. How could I just ignore what I'd learned though?

Finally, as the sun was rising, I gave up on trying to sleep and decided to go home. I snuck out of Mela's room carefully, though I clearly didn't have to worry as her loud snoring went on undisturbed, as well as Steph's soft breathing, and quietly walked down the stairs, heading for the door.

Outside, I was grateful that I had parked on the street and didn't have to back out. I got home, went straight to my room, and climbed into my bed. Once again, I pulled the blankets right up to my ears and put my headphones in and some music on random. It was the only way I could shut off my brain when there was too much on my mind. I just focused on the song, sang the lyrics in my head, and kept doing it until I finally drifted off to sleep.

Several hours later, I woke to a gentle knock at my door. My mom's head peeked in, and I groggily sat up. She entered apprehensively, which I knew meant that she wanted to talk about something but wasn't sure how to bring it up. I had too much on my mind to be gracious about it.

"What's up, Mom?" I spat out a little more harshly than I meant to.

She paused and collected herself before speaking. She did that a lot lately. And when I looked at her tired gray eyes, bone-straight hair, and slumped shoulders, all making her look as though she were carrying the weight of the world, I felt the sting of guilt.

"How was your night? I didn't expect you home this morning," she said quietly.

"It was fine. Steph slept at Mela's too, and they were both snoring so loudly that I couldn't sleep, so I just came home." I shrugged.

"Oh, that makes sense." Again she paused awkwardly, and then went on. "Are you sure you're ready to start at Banting on Monday?"

Not even a little bit, I thought to myself.

"I'll be okay, Mom. I really feel like I can turn over a new leaf there." That was the kind of thing she wanted to hear, and I wanted her not to worry.

"You haven't even looked at the pamphlet, honey." Her voice was full of concern.

True, I hadn't. My new situation would have become more real if I had. I was still hoping for a miraculous time machine to appear so I could undo my mistake.

"I know, Mom, I just..." I trailed off. How would I even start to explain that to her?

"Well, do you want to look at it now?" She pulled out the pamphlet from her pocket.

I sighed but nodded and took it from her.

"It seems like a good school."

I read through the pamphlet quickly, raising my eyebrows in surprise at the school hours.

"School ends before one o'clock there?" I asked incredulously.

"So it would seem." My mom pursed her lips and I nearly laughed.

"What am I going to do with all my free time?"

"Maybe you can get an after-school job, or pick up a new hobby," she suggested warmly.

That wasn't a bad idea, actually. I needed some extra cash for gas money and a trip I had been thinking of taking.

"Yeah, maybe I will," I said slowly.

I continued looking through the school info, and my heart sank when I saw that they had no sports teams. My mom picked up on the shift right away.

"What is it, honey?" she asked, leaning over to look at the pamphlet.

"They don't have any sports."

Running was one of the only times I felt truly free. I had loved being Coach Stewart's favorite. It was the only place I felt like an insider, and now that was gone along with my chances of getting onto the Lion's Track Team. I was sort of glad that I hadn't told my parents about it now. It would only serve to disappoint them even further—if that was even possible at this point.

"Oh, no!" She squeezed my arm sympathetically. "Maybe we can find another option? Or look for a different school?"

"This was our only option, Mom," I mumbled sadly.

"For now." She patted my leg and stood up. I forced myself to smile up at her.

"It'll be okay," I said, with much more enthusiasm than I felt.

There was no need to bring her down with me. I had done this to myself with my reckless behavior, and I was facing the consequences.

She leaned down and kissed the top of my head. "I know it will, sweetie."

12

The weekend passed faster than I expected, and before I knew it I was waking up for school on Monday morning. I had thought about Lucas for most of the time but hadn't come to any real conclusions, other than I felt safe with him and I knew my intuition had never steered me wrong.

I changed my outfit three times before settling on a pair of jeans and a white, long sleeve shirt. I straightened my hair, put on my makeup, and left ten minutes later than I should have, as usual.

The pamphlet of Banting had just shown happy students working independently, and I had no real idea what to expect. I jumped in my car, put the radio on, and changed the station until I found a song I liked and tried to get lost in the music as I drove to my new reality. As I pulled up to the school, I swore under my breath, seeing that there were no pull-through parking spots. Looked like I was leaving late after school.

And I was not prepared for how small Banting was. It didn't look like a school at all. Once I climbed the steps and got inside, arming myself with a deep breath, I was shocked to see that it looked more like a fancy business building with meeting rooms than a high school. Carpeted floors, bright lights, open concept. If it hadn't been for the sign outside, I would have assumed I was in the wrong place—although I still nearly walked back outside to double check. This is not what the pamphlet had led me to think.

I looked around timidly until I saw the receptionist eying me with a small smile. She had dark hair and blue eyes that twinkled mischievously when she smiled. I walked over to her desk.

"Hi there. Are you new here?" Her voice was soft and sweet.

"I am. My name is Olivia Jackson." My throat was so dry that my voice sounded like a croak.

"Ah, the one from Gibbons, right?"

"That's me."

"We don't get many transfers from there. Actually, I think you might be the first."

"Huh," I replied.

She looked at me as though waiting for me to finish my thought—but when it became clear that I had only meant to grunt, she smiled and told me to take a seat. She got on the phone and called someone; I heard "Gibbons" and "transfer" as she spoke quietly to whoever was on the other end.

"Cynthia will see you now."

"Cynthia?" I asked, confused.

"The principal." She said it with a light laugh and pointed to an office.

When I walked over, a woman was waiting. She smiled broadly at me.

"Hi!" she said with enthusiasm. "Welcome to Banting."

"Thanks," I said as I moved slowly to the chair she indicated, across from her desk. I took a seat.

She was an older lady with white hair and kind gray eyes, but I got the feeling that she wasn't a pushover. Her office was a complete disaster, with boxes of files piled high all around and hardly enough space on the desk for her computer.

"So, you are Olivia Jackson?" she asked as she pushed some papers out of the way.

"Yes," I whispered. My hands were shaking. I was now overwhelmed by the thought I had been holding back: that I wasn't ready to start over somewhere new. I had known most people at Gibbons since kindergarten.

"Okay. We have a few ground rules here…"

My stomach tightened, and I braced myself.

"First, if you're a smoker, you can smoke out back. Second, I would appreciate it if you kept any pot off school property. The police come and do random checks from time to time. Third, school starts at nine a.m. and ends at 12:50 p.m., so try to make any appointments you have outside of those times. If you can't avoid it, then just sign yourself out with Cat in front." She pointed to the receptionist as I nodded my understanding.

I was quite surprised that she mentioned pot so nonchalantly. Now the picture of happy students made much more sense to me.

"This is very different from Gibbons," I said with a small smile.

"Oh, I'm sure it is!" She laughed and went on. "This is a great school. We're more relaxed than traditional high schools because the students who come here are not traditional either. Some of them come from rough situations. Some were kicked out of their homes, others have babies, and others had dropped out completely before coming here. What they need is a way for them to get their credits while still being able to work, or care for their kids, or find a place to live."

I sat there nodding, a smile frozen on my face. No one at Gibbons had these kinds of issues. Most of the students there seemed to live perfect lives where the biggest stressors were clothes or boyfriends. I suddenly felt slightly more at home here, knowing that I was going to be among fellow outcasts.

"It's for that reason that everyone who transfers to Banting starts out with the Life Skills course. That's why it took a few weeks to get you in here; we didn't have room in the class yet. You caught the last one before Christmas break, actually."

Ah, that made sense—and also showed me that I had been practically perverse not to have looked at any information about where I was going, and what that might be like. I had been in such a state of confusion and regret that I hadn't wondered about anything at all, not even why I wasn't changing schools with the least loss of time.

I'd just assumed bureaucracy would take time? Or, really, not even thought about anything but my own issues.

Cynthia gave me directions to the Life Skills classroom, and I walked slowly down the hall. Students were milling about the hallway, some reading cross-legged on the floor, others throwing footballs at each other, and others already sitting inside their classrooms, listening to music and ignoring everyone else.

At the end of the hall, I crossed a door that had a paper sign taped to it with the handwritten words "Life-Skills" on it. It was five to nine, but no one was there yet.

The room was painted a very faded blue and had large windows, with lots of light coming in. About fifteen orange plastic chairs formed a circle; no desks anywhere in sight. I had no idea where to sit, but I could hear students coming down the hall, so I quickly scrambled to a chair that faced the door and pulled out a fresh notebook and pen.

I was trying to decide if I should cross my legs or leave them uncrossed when a pimply-faced guy with greasy, dyed blond hair and braces on his teeth walked in. I settled for crossing my ankles and tried to look interested in my blank notebook. He was staring at me, I knew, and he crossed the room to where I was, sitting directly beside me as other students filed in behind him.

"What have we here?" he said loudly.

Awesome. I hated being put on the spot like this. I smiled slightly and tried to ignore him.

"Hellooоо?" He was right in my face. I could hear some people snickering near the door, so I swallowed hard and glared at him.

"Do. You. Speak?" he asked incredibly slowly.

I wanted to die.

"What are you?" he blurted out.

"I'm sorry?" I asked in confusion.

"What's your background? You look Mexican or something." He tilted his head quizzically to the side.

"I'm not sure," I mumbled.

He laughed. "How can you not know what you are?"

"I was adopted, I don't know my background," I said hoping to repress him.

"Huh. Well, you look Mexican to me. That's probably what you are," he decided confidently.

"Yeah, sure. Maybe that's it."

Why some people felt the need to solve the mystery of my background within minutes of meeting me was something I would never understand. I squirmed in my seat as he continued asking me questions I didn't want to answer. The feeling of belonging was long gone, and instead it felt like I had been thrown into a lion's den.

"Eric, why don't you go bother someone else? You're being a douchebag." The female voice came from across the room, and I looked up to see who my savior was.

She was tall, dark, and curvy, with the curliest hair I had ever seen. Eric stood up and muttered "whatever" to himself, but left and went to sit by some guys. The girl came over and took the seat next to me.

"Hey, I'm Cara," she said. "Just ignore Eric. His I.Q. is about the size of this knapsack." She gestured to the bag she had just tossed on the floor, and I snorted.

"I'm Olivia."

"Yeah, I'm not gonna call you that," she said easily. "I'll just call you Liv."

I wanted to say no but I wasn't about to argue with a stranger who seemed disposed to friendliness, so I just nodded my head.

"Thanks for that." I gestured toward Eric.

Cara just smiled knowingly.

"I've been going to school with Eric since I was five. He's basically been an ass ever since."

"Oh, *lovely*," I grumbled, more to myself than anything.

"Don't worry about it, he's harmless." She shrugged her shoulders. "So, what's your deal?" she asked bluntly.

"My deal?"

"Yeah, where did you transfer from? I don't recognize you."

I hesitated to answer her. I had a feeling that being from Gibbons wasn't going to be a ringing endorsement for my character.

"Oh…I transferred from Gibbons," I said finally.

"Gibbons?" She didn't try to mask her surprise.

"Mmmhmm." I stared at my notebook, willing her to change the subject.

"Gibbons girls don't normally wind up here. What'd you do?"

I sighed. She wasn't going to drop it, and I didn't want to alienate myself from anyone this early on. I knew I had to give her something. "I punched a girl in the face, so I got expelled." I said it quietly so that other people didn't overhear.

"Whoa! I would have never pegged you for the violent type." She sounded impressed, which made me grimace.

"I'm not usually."

Her eyes burned with curiosity. "Did she deserve it?"

"Definitely," I said without hesitation.

Cara smirked and nodded her head in satisfaction.

"You're all right with me, Liv."

I returned her smile shyly. I wasn't used to making friends with other girls so easily. More students had come in while we were talking, and the seats were mostly filled. A lady entered suddenly, and she didn't dress like a teacher normally would, so I wasn't sure if she was the teacher or just a mature student.

"All right, guys, settle down," she said with mild annoyance; definitely the teacher, then.

"My name is Leslie Anne Rowland, but you can call me LA. This class is called Life Skills because my guess is a lot of you are lacking them."

I snickered under my breath as she walked around the room while she spoke.

"You need to prove that you're ready to be here because I don't want to waste my time, or yours. This class is four weeks long and during those four weeks, we will create your resume since some of you need to get a job right now. We will figure out what kind of career you want to go into so that you have some kind of vision for your lives instead of simply existing from day to day, stoned and confused." She seemed to look directly at Eric at that last comment which immediately made me like her.

"Because no one has ever believed in some of you, and through a series of terrible choices that YOU have made, this is where you ended up. I would prefer not to see any of my students behind bars so let's start making some new choices, shall we?"

I had never heard a teacher speak that way before. She spoke to us as though we were adults in charge of our own lives instead of children who needed to be constantly herded. It felt empowering in a way. She continued.

"Respect is earned, not freely given. If you respect me, I will respect you. I believe in each and every one of you. I believe in your ability to graduate. I believe in your ability to do great things with your lives. Most of all, I believe in your ability to believe in yourselves. You have greatness in you, let's figure out where to focus it."

A stillness reigned in the room for a few moments, and I was sure someone was going to break out into a slow, ironic clap. Instead, the moment passed, and Eric belched.

"Thanks for that contribution, Eric," LA said while he took a mock bow. The room erupted into the normal classroom sounds and Cara leaned over to me.

"Well, that was lame," she muttered.

I gave a little laugh to seem like I agreed but that speech had spoken directly to my soul. For the first time in a long time, I felt like just maybe I was going to be okay.

13

The week passed by uneventfully. I showed up for class, avoided the massive clouds of cigarette smoke outside by staying in for every break, and hung around after school until I was sure everyone had left so no one would hear my backup beeper. It didn't take too long; the students at Banting never lingered after class. Eric stayed away from me, and I sat beside Cara every day. She was really growing on me. She was full of confidence, the kind of girl who assumed that everyone wanted to be her friend. She was exactly the type of person I needed around.

The only exception to my hiding out in the classroom was my annoyingly small bladder forcing me to take regular bathroom breaks. You didn't have to ask to go pee at Banting, which was a welcome change. The first time I asked LA to be excused she just stared at me, rolled her eyes, and went on a diatribe against the idiocy of traditional high schools and their antiquated bathroom rules.

It was Friday morning and I had a job interview at Brew before school, so I was up extra early. I grabbed my school stuff, hopped in the car, and ten minutes later I pulled into Brew's parking lot. I checked my makeup quickly in the mirror and once satisfied, I went inside for my interview. I was meeting with Sara something or other. As I approached the counter, there was only one person working.

"Hi, are you Sara?" I asked nervously.

"Yes, ma'am. Are you Olivia?"

"I sure am!" I responded enthusiastically. It definitely didn't feel natural to sound so peppy, but I really wanted the job and it was hard to get hired with a standoffish demeanor. A line was forming quickly, and I stood out of the way.

"Sorry, Olivia," she said while she expertly grabbed coffees and made cappuccinos. "Someone was supposed to come in to help me this morning but he's late," she said with a slight frown.

"Oh, no worries at all. Is there anything I can do to help?" I didn't actually think I'd be much help, but it felt rude not to at least offer.

"Bless you, sweet thing. Just give me five minutes, and I'm sure we can do a quick interview."

I nodded and took a seat out of the way.

Sara seemed nice. She was a good ten years older than I, and was clearly very experienced in the industry. She had blonde hair and bright blue eyes. After a few minutes, a nerdy-looking guy with glasses and a baseball cap ran into the store and immediately walked behind the counter, tying his apron as he went.

"You're late," Sara said tersely through her teeth while she continued smiling at the customer she was serving.

"I know, I know. I'm sorry."

She gave him a light punch in the arm and let him take over. Coming my way, she sat down across from me.

"Sorry, hon. So, have you ever worked before?" she asked, eyeing me suspiciously.

"Well, no not exactly. But I'm a quick learner, I'm responsible, and I have great availability."

I beamed at her, hoping that she would overlook my lack of experience. She looked over a resume that detailed some babysitting and other odd jobs I had done.

"Okay, I like you, so I'll give you a shot. When can you start?"

We worked out a schedule for the following two weeks. On my way out and to school, I texted Mela the news that I got the job, and she wrote back quickly suggesting that we go out for a celebratory dinner. I agreed.

The entire drive to school my thoughts went back and forth: I was excited about my new job, but disappointed that Lucas hadn't called. I was so not the girl who stared at her phone waiting for some guy to call, but that's exactly what I had been doing all week.

"Earth to Liv…" Cara's voice broke through my thoughts in the classroom.

I snapped back to attention and responded quickly. "Sorry, what's up?"

"Where have you been for the last twenty minutes? You've barely responded to anything I've said."

I hadn't even realized she was talking to me. "I'm sorry! Just tired from getting up so early, I guess." I grimaced.

The end of class was nearing and I started gathering my things, sneaking a quick glance at my phone. Still nothing.

"You've been obsessively checking that thing all week. Who is blowing you off?" she asked knowingly.

"No one. I just…" I hesitated. Did I really want to talk to her about Lucas? I hadn't even told Mela how much it was bothering me.

"Just what? Spill." She turned in her chair to face me. I sighed.

"I met a guy last weekend and…I thought he'd text, but he hasn't." It sounded so pathetic out loud.

"Aww man, that sucks."

"I know, right?" I said with frustration. "You think you have a connection with someone and then you wonder if you made it up entirely in your head."

"You should just call him," she suggested. I looked at her with alarm. She laughed. "Or not…"

There were no bells at Banting. LA just waved her hand dismissively.

"See you on Monday, everyone! Don't do anything stupid," she said with a mix of enthusiasm and sarcasm. She was by far the best teacher I had ever had.

"You hiding out in here until the coast is clear?" Cara asked as she stood up. I nodded sheepishly. "I've gotta hear that beeper sometime."

She wished me a good weekend. I smiled and waved as I sat in my seat and waited for everyone to clear out.

It wasn't until I was practically at my car door that I noticed someone leaning against it. A knot appeared in my throat thinking it might be Chris. I looked up and almost dropped my bag when I saw that it was Lucas.

"Hey!" I said with surprise. A slow, crooked smile, spread across his face and it made my heart leap.

"Hey," he said with a hint of reservation.

"What are you doing here?" I asked.

He laughed easily. "I go here."

What? How was that possible? I'd been there all week and hadn't seen him once.

"For how long?" I asked dazedly.

"I started in September."

"I'm surprised we haven't seen each other, I've been here all week."

"Oh, I've seen you. I just didn't say anything."

"Oh!" I couldn't hide my shock. How could he have seen me all week and not said hello?

"Look I have to go, I'm going to be late." I pulled my car door open, forcing him to move out of the way.

"Hey, I just—"

"No, it's fine. I get it, Lucas. I'll see ya." I slid into the driver's seat, slammed my door, and pulled out of the parking spot leaving him standing there looking after me. I cringed as the sound of the backup beeper seemed to reverberate throughout the parking lot.

All week I had sat there like an idiot, checking my phone every two seconds, and he couldn't so much as say hello? He probably *did* have a girlfriend. I felt so stupid. I should have never let him get into my head like that. At least I knew I could avoid seeing him for the rest of the year just by continuing what I'd been doing all week.

I went home to kill time before meeting up with Mela. I spent the rest of the afternoon texting back and forth with her, and she was dutifully outraged on my behalf. At least I could just move on, I kept telling myself. The problem was, I wasn't convincing anyone—least of all myself.

14

Mela and I were meeting up at a local burger joint because they had the best food and gave us a mountain of fries. I had arrived there first, which almost never happened. Once I had been seated in a booth facing the door, I pulled my phone out to text Mela.

Where are you?

I could see that she was typing, which either meant that she was here or hadn't even left yet.

Don't hate me but I'm not coming.

Not coming? She wasn't the blow-off kind of friend. I immediately wrote back.

What? Why? This was your idea!

I know, but he begged me.

He who?

A name popped up on my phone just as the door opened.

Lucas.

He stood in the doorway hesitantly, wearing jeans and a light blue t-shirt. I was about to run for the bathroom, but he saw me and walked quickly over to me.

"You didn't let me explain," he said in a low voice as he slid into the booth opposite me.

"I didn't need an explanation," I responded coolly while shifting uncomfortably in my seat.

"You've got me all figured out, then, have you?" He sounded annoyed as he ran a hand through his hair.

Good, so was I. "I don't know, you tell me."

"Are you hungry?" he asked. I was confused by his sudden change of direction, and for a second I thought he meant hangry. I was starving, after having lost my appetite all day.

"Umm—yeah, actually," I mumbled.

He asked me what I wanted and went to place the order. When I moved to grab some money, he shook his head. I began to wonder if maybe I had been wrong about him. I supposed I at least owed him a few minutes. I needed to stop cutting people out of my life so easily. He came back with two burgers, two massive piles of fries, ketchup, mayo, and bbq sauce.

"I wasn't sure which one you liked best," he said with a smile.

I took the mayo and bbq sauce and mixed them together. He sat down across from me again and I started nibbling on my fries.

"So," he started, "I don't have a girlfriend."

I wondered how he knew what I had been thinking and decided that I would need to remind Mela of the girl code.

"Okay," I said quietly.

"I haven't called you because, honestly, I wasn't sure if you wanted me to."

I raised my eyebrows and he put his hands up in defense.

"Hear me out!" he cried.

I motioned for him to go on as I nibbled nervously on some more fries.

"When I met you that day on the beach, we had this instant connection, but you didn't give me your number. Then when I saw you that night at the beach party, I couldn't believe my luck, but you practically ran away from me when you saw me standing with Nate."

I had really been hoping he hadn't seen that; I was mortified.

"Then we hung out...and I thought we had a great time, but you still didn't give me your number. When I saw you at school, I didn't know what to do. I was hoping to catch your eye, but you barely left your class—and when you did, you were always checking your phone."

My cheeks were on fire.

"I finally got the nerve to talk to you today because I figured it was Friday, so if you blew me off at least I'd have the weekend to recover. You were so mad and I didn't know why, so I begged Nate to ask Mela. When I found out you thought I had a girlfriend, I needed to see you to explain. I'm really sorry." His eyes pleaded with me.

Now he was apologizing? I was officially a terrible person. He was right on all accounts; I just hadn't realized how observant he was.

"No, don't apologize, Lucas. I'm the one who should be apologizing to you." I winced.

He looked puzzled. I guess I deserved that.

"I do like you, I just...I don't know. I don't know what's wrong with me."

I'm not sure what I expected him to do, but he caught me off guard by flashing me a grin. I sat there staring at him, caught myself, and continued eating my fries.

"So..." I looked up at him. "You like me?"

He widened his grin. I choked on my fries and started coughing.

"I'm not saying it again," I said through coughs.

Smiling playfully, he handed me my drink. We ate the rest of our food in comfortable silence while I tried, unsuccessfully, not to eat my burger like a savage. I was so hungry that I finished before he did. I sat across from him, tapping my foot and waiting for him to finish.

I wasn't sure what would happen next. Would we keep hanging out? Maybe he had other plans. Maybe I should act like I had other plans. Before I could overthink things too much, he was throwing out our garbage and walking back toward me.

"Do you want to get out of here?"

His hand was extended toward me again. I smiled up at him. It was basically his signature move now. I didn't know where we were going, but I suddenly didn't care; I grabbed his hand and followed him out. Outside, he turned to me with excited eyes.

"Can I take you to one of my favorite spots?" I looked over and saw that he had borrowed Nate's truck.

"Sure, sounds fun." I was trying to sound laid back.

He smirked as though he saw right through me and unlocked my door while helping me up into the truck. Feeling his warm hand on my back sent a shock through my entire body. How did he *do* that? His door was still locked, and I reached over to unlock it for him. He smiled at me as though that simple act was vital.

As soon as we pulled out of the parking lot, he reached shyly for my hand. I let him hold it. Whenever we were together, I just wanted to be close to him. I had no idea where we were headed, but before long we pulled into a forested area that looked like it was off-limits.

Lucas turned toward me.

"Do you trust me?" he asked as he waggled his eyebrows.

"Umm, should I?" I responded hesitantly. The truth was, though, I knew he wouldn't hurt me.

"I promise it'll be worth it."

The sun had just set, and it was dark in the forest. We walked hand in hand through the woods for several minutes. The path wasn't clearly defined, but I could tell it had been traveled on more than once. He slowed his pace and turned to me.

"Are you ready?"

With no idea as to what to expect, I just nodded. He pulled me through several trees and I gasped. We were standing on the edge of a huge body of water that seemed to sparkle. I quickly realized that the sparkles were coming from hundreds and hundreds of fireflies that were floating majestically above the water. Their little lights twinkled as they turned on and off, and the entire lake was surrounded by cliffs that protected it from the outside. It was easily one of the most beautiful sights I had ever seen. I could hardly believe I had never been there, considering I'd lived twenty minutes away for almost my entire life.

"What *is* this place?" I asked in disbelief.

"It's called Pink Lake. It was named after the Pink family, who settled here in the 1800s." He added that last part after seeing the confused look on my face.

The lake definitely wasn't pink. I couldn't quite tell what color it was because of how dark it was getting, but it was beautiful. He took a few steps and sat on a massive flat rock. I looked at it apprehensively, realizing that I would have to climb up to reach it. He laughed at the look on my face, and I extended my hands to let him pull me up. He did it so effortlessly that I was taken aback. He was a lot stronger than I had realized. But when he put his arm around me and I rested my head on his shoulder, it felt so natural to be with him.

"You ok?" His words surprised me because I was perfectly happy at the moment.

"Yeah, I'm good."

He shifted so that he was looking into my eyes. "Are *we* okay?"

"We're good," I said with a smile.

He seemed to relax. We spent the next few hours talking and getting to know each other better. I confided in him how much I liked running for the track team and how sad I was that Banting didn't have one.

"I think the city has a track team that anyone over sixteen can try out for. That's what I did with football since I couldn't play for Fort Lauderdale High anymore."

That sounded hopeful. "Oh, yeah? I'll have to look into that."

A while later, he finally told me about his complicated relationship with his family and how he hadn't seen his dad since he was three.

"Is that hard for you?" I asked him, surprising myself. I didn't normally pry.

"It kind of is what it is. I think he drinks a lot. My mom puts up with a lot more than she should, and if she left him and fled with us, then things must have been pretty bad. Still, though, a part of me wants to find him."

I confessed that I knew about Mela picking him up that day. He wasn't surprised.

"I figured she would have told you. I was surprised you didn't already know at the party."

"I guess she respected Nate enough to stay quiet when he asked her not to tell anyone."

He nodded his agreement.

"Have you been back since?" I asked gently.

"A couple of times. I asked her to choose between me and her abusive boyfriend of the month. She chose him."

"I'm sorry."

He shrugged. We sat quietly for a while then he broke the silence.

"Have you ever wanted to find your birth parents?" His voice was barely above a whisper.

This was the hardest thing to talk about, and I never did—yet I knew I could trust him. I opened my mouth to answer him, but nothing came out.

"I'm sorry, you don't have to answer that."

"No, no. It's not that," I stammered.

What was it then? He was staring at me, and I could feel my face getting hot. He sat there, quietly waiting me out. A few more minutes passed, while I realized that I simply did not know how to speak of it, like someone might not know how to speak a word in an obscure foreign language—but then the words finally came.

"My mom has always kept in touch with my birth mother through letters. She asks about me sometimes, and my mom keeps her updated," I started.

"She doesn't write to you?" he asked.

"Not directly no," It was nice that he thought it was weird too. "To be fair, it's not like I write to her either."

"Well, yeah. But she's the parent here, not you."

He wasn't wrong.

"I sometimes wonder if she cares more about my mom's feelings than mine," I confessed quietly. "But maybe that's unfair of me."

"I don't think it's unfair, but there's only one way to know for sure," he replied softly. I turned and looked at him questioningly. "Ask her."

My heart sped up at the mere thought, but I knew that he was right. It was an easy answer, and yet it felt so complicated. What if I was right? It felt safer to stay in the dark—but I knew I would always wonder.

"Maybe I will," I said uncertainly.

He leaned back and rested on the palms of his hands. The silence stretched before us as we gazed at the fireflies.

"I think I do want to go and see her," I finally said quietly.

"Yeah?"

"Yeah. I've been thinking about it for a while. It's actually why I got a job. I just feel like…" I trailed off.

"Feel like what?" he asked cautiously. Maybe it was because

it was so dark and I could hardly see him, but I suddenly felt brave.

"I feel like I'm not a whole person. I've never met her or her family, I don't know half of my history… How am I supposed to know who I am if I don't even know where I came from?" I whispered the last part. I had never told anyone that before, not even Mela.

His voice and eyes were soft. "That makes sense."

"It does?" I didn't want him to think I was a total freak.

"Yeah, for sure. I mean, I kind of feel like that too sometimes. Just…lost."

Tears filled my eyes so quickly I couldn't stop them. I silently brushed them away, hoping he wouldn't notice.

"Well, if you need a friend to go with you, I'm available." He smiled.

"Thanks. Is that what we are?"

"Something like that."

He looked in my eyes and slowly leaned toward me. He stopped just inches away from my face and waited. I wasn't afraid anymore. I smiled and leaned toward him and he pressed his lips gently against mine. It felt like a thousand fireworks went off inside my chest. I was trying to control my breathing as he smiled, pulled back, and kept the conversation lighthearted.

It was as though we had crammed a decade of friendship into a few hours, but I barely felt the time pass. Being with him was like being with someone I had known forever. When he finally drove me home, he reminded me to think about his offer: He'd come with me to meet my birth mother. I promised I would consider it, and I meant it. The more I got to know him, the more I wanted to spend time with him and even though it scared me to death—I felt like he might be worth the risk.

After Lucas dropped me off, I lay in bed awake most of the night, thinking about whether or not to go see my birth mother. Did I really want to meet her? I knew she had gotten married and had a couple more kids. It might be such a strange experience. I thought about all the reasons to go and the many more not to. The excitement I'd felt earlier was long gone, and now I felt ridiculous for even considering it.

It was a stupid idea. Nothing good can come of it, I should just call the whole thing off.

I wrestled with my feelings until three a.m., and eventually drifted off into a very restless sleep.

15

Before I knew it, Thanksgiving week was upon us. After my talk with Lucas about running for the city, I had sent coach Stewart an e-mail asking if he thought that might be a way to keep the scout interested in me.

Olivia,

It's so nice to hear from you! Yes, I think that's a wonderful idea. Tryouts are in January, so in the meantime keep up your training. There's a track by Moorewood Park you can use, and I'll e-mail you the weekly practices I'm doing with the team. Once you make the city team, I'll inform the scout of the change. I haven't said anything about what happened, and it shouldn't affect your chances.

Rooting for you,

Coach Stewart

A smile slowly spread across my face as I read his words and then read through once more to make sure I hadn't imagined it.

"What are you smiling about?" Lucas's voice interrupted my thoughts. We were sitting on the grass outside of Banting with Cara, who lay on a blanket sunbathing in shorts and a tank top.

"My old coach is going to send me their practices so that I can keep up on my training." I smiled.

"That's *good* news?" Cara remarked with a laugh while lifting her head just to raise her eyebrows at me.

I smirked at her. "Yes, it's good news. This way I can try out for the city team in January and still have a chance to impress the scout who was coming to see me."

I hadn't told Lucas about that when we talked because I didn't think it was still possible, and I was tired of feeling sad about it.

"A scout? For what?" he asked curiously.

"He was going to offer me a spot on the Lion's," I said timidly.

He whistled. "That's huge! You must be even faster than I thought. I can't believe you didn't tell me the other night. That is phenomenal." He looked at me with admiration. I blushed.

"Running ain't my thing but good on ya, girl! That sounds like a big deal." Cara gave me a thumbs up from her spot on the blanket.

I couldn't help but compare Lucas's reaction to Chris's. What a difference between them. Chris had been worried about how it would affect my time for him, and Lucas couldn't be happier for me. I realized then that this was the first time I had even thought about Chris in a while. Maybe I was turning the corner. I hoped so.

"What are you guys doing for thanksgiving?" I asked, hoping to get the focus off of me.

"Not a thing," Cara mumbled.

I was surprised. "Nothing?"

"Nah, my dad's new wife is a bee-otch and they're all going to her family's place for dinner. I opted out." She was leaning up on her elbows and shrugged easily.

"Oh man, that sucks. What about you, Lucas?" Thinking of his complicated family life, I immediately wished I hadn't asked.

"I'm just gonna lay low in my room at Nate's. They're all going to his grandparents and they invited me, but I'd rather just stay back." He forced a smile.

"What about you, Liv?" Cara asked.

"Well, my mom's a vegetarian, so normally I'd enjoy the delights of some tofurkey but my parents are flying out to visit with my brothers. I'm on my own too."

"Sounds kind of like you dodged a tofurkey bullet to me," Cara said snidely, making us all laugh. She wasn't wrong; it was disgusting. I couldn't remember the last time I had eaten a real turkey dinner.

"What if we made our own Thanksgiving?" Lucas suggested after a moment.

"What do you have in mind?" I couldn't cook to save my life.

"Nate's parents actually bought everything to cook dinner themselves, but then their plans changed. They told me I was welcome to all the food, but I wasn't about to cook an entire turkey dinner for myself."

"You cook?" Cara asked with surprise.

"Yeah, I do, actually." He smiled. Boy, the charm on him…

"Could I invite a few people from school? I know some peeps who have nothing going on too and might like an invite." Cara nodded her head toward Banting.

"Of course, the more the merrier."

He leaned back on his elbows while I watched him carefully. He cooked, was always so encouraging, made me feel safe, and certainly wasn't hard to look at. He caught my eye and winked. Yes, I was definitely in trouble.

IN THE END, there were seven of us. Cara and Lucas, of course, and once Mela found out about the alternative Thanksgiving, she wasn't about to be left out. She and Nate changed their plans. Then Isabel and Adam came too. I wasn't entirely clear on what they were to each other, but I knew for sure they were friends, and I had seen them around school.

"Can I help with anything?" I asked Lucas for the third time.

Everything smelled heavenly, and he had been cooking all day. He gave me a look and offered to let me whip up the potatoes, which I gladly took him up on. He got the beaters out for me and drained the potatoes, then put them back in the pot for me to mash. Once I was done, I sat at the large island, watching as he took the turkey out of the oven. It was baked to perfection.

"Where did you learn how to cook like this?" I asked in awe. He smiled at me and came over to lean against the island.

"My mom used to teach me before—" He paused and looked embarrassed. I waited, and he went on. "Before she decided that getting high was more important than parenting. I guess I absorbed the cooking lessons well enough."

He looked off for a minute before shaking his head and smiling down at me. I reached for him and pulled him into a hug. We stayed like that for a while, until a timer went off for the veggies. He pulled away after kissing the top of my head.

I helped him lay everything out on the island as everyone else sat in the living room and chatted. I smiled at the laughter and camaraderie among this small group of misfits. All of us coming from different backgrounds and walks of life and barely knowing each other—but somehow, the gathering worked.

"Come and get it!" Lucas called to the group.

Everyone made their way into the kitchen sniffing appreciatively and not hesitating to fill up their plates.

"Dang, Lucas, you can cook!" Cara called out with her mouth full.

Mela gave me a wink that essentially said, *You'd better marry him someday,* which made me giggle. I filled my plate with turkey, stuffing, mashed potatoes, and corn and then slathered gravy on it all. Nate had pulled a large coffee table close to the couch; we all sat around it, eating and talking.

I learned that Isabel and Adam were in fact just friends who lived together after being kicked out of their homes.

"Wow, I'm sorry," I mumbled.

Isabel tossed her long light brown hair over her shoulder.

"Oh it's fine, we make do. We both have jobs. We share a one-bedroom apartment, and this gentleman insists that I take the bedroom while he sleeps on the couch."

She gave Adam a playful elbow and he smiled bashfully. He had boyish features and curly blond hair, but he had a way about him that made him seem much older than he looked.

"Of course! Like I was gonna hog the bedroom when soon there'll be two of you."

She looked down at her stomach. I hadn't noticed the bump before, but now it was all I could see. My food suddenly became harder to swallow.

"Who's the baby daddy?" Cara asked bluntly. Trust her to get right to the point. Isabel's eyes looked wistful now.

"He's gone." She shrugged. "Anyway, once my parents found out, they kicked me to the curb. Typical."

She took another bite of food. Lucas caught my eye. I wondered if this is what my birth parents had dealt with before I was born.

"Are you going to keep…it?" I whispered, shocking myself at the forward question.

"Her. And yes, I am. She belongs with me. And since I have Adam, I know I won't be alone."

Her eyes were full of determination. It made me sad to think of my birth mother alone and pregnant. From what I had heard, she had been asked to leave too. As if that would actually solve anything.

"To friends," Nate said quietly as he raised his glass of sparkling apple cider. We each followed suit and raised our glasses as well.

"To friends," we all repeated in unison.

16

After that misfit Thanksgiving, all I could think about was whether or not to send my birth mother an e-mail asking if I could come and see her. Lucas strongly encouraged it, and just as Isabel had seemed to draw strength from Adam, I felt like I was drawing strength from him.

I had written and deleted about fifty versions of the e-mail never quite working up the courage to hit send until I realized that I was running late for work. I stared at the keys on my laptop and took a deep breath.

Dear Ali,

Hi, it's Olivia, your daughter. I was wondering if I could come and meet you? It's something that I've been thinking of for a while now and would really like to make it happen.

Please let me know what you think.

Olivia

The mouse was shaking as I looked at the screen. I looked down at my sweaty hands and realized that I was the one shaking. *What am I doing? What if she hates me? What if she says no?*

A tiny voice in the back of my mind was asking, *What if she says yes, though?*

I needed to get to work. I took a deep breath and clicked

send. Then I pushed back from my desk and stood up quickly. *What did I just do?* I only had time to grab my purse and head out the door.

That was probably why I had chosen to do this now; I couldn't be late for work, and I wouldn't be able to sit there thinking one thing and its opposite a million times.

Now it was done. I had leaped.

I got into my car and took another deep breath. *It's gonna be fine.* It was now or never, do or die, make or break. A hundred more clichés ran through my head as I put the car in reverse.

Beep, beep, beep.

The incessant beeping of my back up beeper was so loud, it was ramming into my brain.

Beep – she's not going to like you.

Beep – this is a huge mistake.

Beep – if she wanted you around, she would've kept you the way Isabel is keeping her baby.

The last thought made me slam the car into drive halfway down my driveway and pull forward right over the last bit of our neighbor's grass. Unfortunately for me, he was standing outside and raising his arms in disbelief while shaking his fist at me. I cringed and waved an apology but didn't stop.

I needed to disable that stupid beeper, or I was going to go nuts. Visions of ripping out the wires one by one entertained me all the way to work. Distracted, I pulled right up to Brew and parked before remembering that I needed a pull-through spot. I threw my head back and groaned in frustration as I gripped the steering wheel tightly in an attempt to calm down. Why was I panicking about this? I tried to think of something calming but nothing came to mind. Sighing, I gave up and went in to work.

My shift passed fairly quickly. I was grateful for the hustle and bustle of the busy coffee shop. It helped keep my mind off of the e-mail I very much regretted sending. And Sara was generously taking on a sixteen-year-old girl; I didn't want to let her down.

During my break, I sent Lucas a text asking if he could meet with me after work. He was the only one who knew I was even thinking about going to see Ali. I figured that maybe he could talk me off of this ledge.

Of course. Everything ok?

My eyes began pricking with tears, so I squeezed my lids shut and held my breath until the sensation went away.

Not really.

It was as forthcoming as I could get for the moment. I didn't want to breakdown at work, so I shoved my phone in my pocket and tried not to think about anything for the rest of my shift.

Brew was rustic and cool, with shelves of books for the patrons to read while they had their drinks, and I just watched them coming and going, slowly drinking and savoring their beverages, sometimes coming up for a refill or a pastry. Their movements and their calm made me feel better, as if everything could be taken with as much calm.

Until I got back into my car after work and checked my e-mail. There was one from Ali.

With shaking hands, I opened it and started to read.

Dear Olivia,

Have you talked to your parents about this? I wouldn't want to step on any toes. Do you think they're okay with this idea? If yes, then perhaps we can plan a time to meet.

Sincerely,

Ali

I stared at my phone in frustration and then tossed it onto the passenger seat in disgust. Putting the car in reverse, I backed out as quickly as I could without slamming into anything.

Beep – see? She cares more about their feelings than yours.

Beep – this was a bad idea from the start. You only have yourself to blame.

Beep – she didn't want you then, why would she want you now?

I slammed the car into drive and narrowly missed hitting an oncoming truck. The blaring horn snapped me back to reality, and once I managed to get my heart and my breathing under control, I forced myself to focus on driving.

Lucas and I were to meet at Nate's since he was basically living there. As soon as my headlights lit up the enormous house, I saw him sitting outside on the large interlock porch, waiting for me. He stood up right away, walked over to my car, and opened my door for me.

"What happened?" he asked immediately, concern in his eyes.

"That stupid back up beeper is driving me insane!" I said angrily as I shoved my phone in my purse and got out of the car.

"Okay…*that's* what bothering you?"

"Yes! It's so freaking annoying, I just want to rip my car apart!" I slammed the door, gave it a kick for good measure, and stormed over to the front porch with Lucas behind me.

"Do you want to talk about it?"

I whipped around. "Talk about what?"

He was quiet for a moment, in that way he had, his hands in his pockets. Then he said, "Talk about what's really bothering you."

"That *is* what's bothering me! The stupid beeps are so loud I can't even hear myself think. And why did you talk me into sending Ali an e-mail? I knew it was going to be a disaster."

"Ali?"

"My birth mother," I shot back in frustration. "I knew she was going to write back with some asinine response but still I walked right into the trap anyway." I sank down on the step and put my head in my hands.

Well, I guess now he knows what's really bothering me…

"What did she say?" he asked softly.

I dug my phone out of my purse angrily and handed it to him, the e-mail already onscreen. I waited for him to say something, but he stayed silent. Eventually, I snuck a glance at him; he was still staring at my phone, his eyes narrowed ever so slightly.

"What do you think?" I mumbled into my knees hesitantly.

He took a minute to answer. "I think maybe she's being cautious since your parents have kept the door open for her." He looked at me. "It's not the most inviting email but perhaps she's just as nervous as you."

"Or maybe this is all a huge mistake." I was still talking to my knees.

He sat down next to me. "You don't have to do this you know."

"Of course I do," I murmured after swallowing hard. All the fight had left me, and I felt drained. I looked at him helplessly and understanding dawned on his face. He simply nodded. I watched the muscles in his jaw clench and unclench a few times before he spoke again.

"Do you want to come in for a bit?" His voice was barely above a whisper. "No one is here…"

"Okay." I sounded resigned but I was too tired to care. We stood up, and I followed him into the house.

In the living room, I sat on the gray sectional beside him. He turned on the TV, and we watched in hypnotized silence as a game show played. Bright lights, bright colors, bright smiles, bright voices. All had to be well, right? Nothing could be so bad.

We just kept on going right into another show, and I snuggled closer, laying my head and arm over his chest. His heart didn't seem like mine; it seemed steady. Mine was a drum of war, his was quiet music. He rubbed my arm softly, and I tried not to think about what I was going to say in response to Ali. After the show, it was starting to get late.

"I should get going," I said. "Curfew."

"Sure. Why don't I go and start your car for you? It's kind of chilly," he offered.

Wordlessly I handed him the keys and stood up to put my sweater on. As I waited for him to return, I sauntered over to the massive bookcase. It must have had a thousand books on it. Between the stone fireplace in the corner and the ladder on the bookshelf, I had always loved this room. I fought the urge to jump onto the ladder and swing from one side to the other. I wondered if Nate had ever done that as a child. His parents seemed laid back enough that they would have let him.

His family was so different from mine. Loaded for one, which was basically the opposite of mine. Nate's mom was a famous author, and his dad owned some kind of finance company. Even though they were rich, they weren't stuck up about it. They resembled an after school special, but not in a cheesy way. I guessed that was why Nate was so easily able to let things roll off his back. Nothing seemed to faze him, but when the chips were down? He was always there. With candy.

A few minutes later Lucas came back in, rubbing his hands together.

"Brrr!" he exclaimed loudly. He laughed at the look on my face. I despised the cold.

As I followed him out to my car, I suddenly wished that I hadn't dumped all of my negativity on him.

"I'm sorry about tonight, Lucas," I said with a grimace.

"You have nothing to apologize for."

He pulled me into a hug. I shivered into his chest as I hugged him back.

Unzipping his jacket, He pulled my arms around his waist inside of it. I was instantly ten times warmer. I just breathed him in. It had been a rough day so far, but this made up for it.

When I looked up at him, he was smiling down at me. He leaned in slowly and I made up the distance by pressing my lips to his. He seemed pleasantly surprised as he pulled me closer and kissed me deeper than the last time. Tingles shot straight up my spine the longer the kiss went on. By the end of it, we were both breathing heavily. Putting his forehead against mine, he cleared his throat.

"Umm…goodnight, then."

"Goodnight," I added with a wink, "Thanks for keeping me warm."

He laughed. It felt like the cloud of despair was beginning to lift.

"See you at school, beautiful," he whispered in my ear.

I simply nodded, not trusting myself to get past the lump in my throat to say anything. I got into my car, grateful that it was so warm, and waited until Lucas went back inside to put it into reverse. He just stood at the door with his arms crossed and waited for me to back out with a mischievous grin on his face. I shook my head and pointed for him to go inside; he refused. I wondered how long he was prepared to stand there, waiting to hear the backup beeper.

As if reading my mind, he sat down on the steps and made himself comfortable. Once more I shook my head and grimaced, then put the car in reverse. To my shock, there was no beeping. I looked up at him in disbelief as he held up a pair of scissors with a smile so wide I thought it might light up the entire sky. He must have disabled the beeper when he'd come out to start my car.

Laughing out loud, I blew him a kiss of gratitude and took my time backing out. I gave him one last wave and watched him in the rear-view mirror as I drove away. At home, when I put the car in park, I checked my phone and saw that there was a text from him.

Now you won't have to go crazy.

I was smiling so hard my cheeks hurt. He had been able to

turn a bad night around, and I couldn't remember that ever happening before. I wrote him back to let him know I was home safe. As I crawled into bed, my phone lit up.

Sweet dreams.

17

My lungs were screaming for air. It felt like every muscle in my body was about to collapse but I refused to give in.

I had been running through the exercises coach Stewart had given me for over an hour. Burpees, bounding, high knees, butt kicks, sprints; the list was extensive. I secretly wondered if this was really the practice he had scheduled for everyone else, or if he was making sure I stayed in shape. Regardless, I did everything on the list several times.

The track at Moorewood Park wasn't as good as the one at Gibbons, but it was better than nothing. Instead of rubber beneath my feet, there was loose gravel. The stones went flying as I did my exercises, and more than once I was given a snooty look by the powerwalking ladies. Nothing seemed quite as ridiculous in my eyes than middle-aged women pumping their arms dramatically with absolutely no speed. What was the point?

Two more women strode past me in matching track suits, arms pumping furiously. I bit back the laugh that threatened to escape my lips. I knew I should be getting ready to cool down, and though my muscles were begging me to give it a rest, my mind was still racing. I took off down the track, determined to beat my own time again.

To meet Ali or not, that was the question. My mind wasn't made up. I had never felt so pulled toward a stranger and so terrified of her all at the same time. It might turn out wonderful, or it might be the biggest mistake of my life. Any way I looked at it, the decision would be a gamble.

I figured that Mela and Nate would come with me, and of course Lucas had offered. But was I ready for such a monumental adventure? Maybe I had been through enough this year and should just give myself time. Or maybe this was exactly what I needed to feel like me again. Still, I couldn't decide, and my hesitation was starting to make me furious.

The wind whipped through my hair as I sprinted. I blew by the matching track suits and heard their cries of alarm. My shins burned with pain from running on such a crappy surface, and I knew I should stop. The last thing I needed were shin splints.

Allowing myself to slow down, I jogged easily around the entire track and my breathing returned to a normal pace. Out of the corner of my eye I saw a black Camaro drive by slowly; before I could help it, my head whipped around to follow it. But it continued driving without stopping, and I let the breath I didn't know I was holding out. *Not every Camaro has Chris behind the wheel.*

Whenever I saw a black car now, I was gripped by sudden panic. Would it ever stop? I walked over to my stuff on the grass, took a long drink of my water, and stopped long enough to send a quick e-mail to Coach Stewart, letting him know I had completed his list. He was still rooting for me, and I was determined not to let him, or myself, down.

Weaving through the children playing in the park, I crossed through the field to get home faster. The black car had made me uneasy, and I needed to get out of the public eye. But the pain in my shins increased; I was forced to drop down onto the grass to stretch. I had wanted to wait until I got home, but I didn't have that luxury anymore.

The playground was busy, with people strolling the path or kicking soccer balls in the field. The children either played with their parents or called to them, to show them some wonderful feat, even if it was just going down the slide. Mothers smiled and clapped. A father pretended to be amazed when his son, who didn't reach the top of his hip, gave a heartfelt but wobbly kick to a ball. A couple of children fell and began to cry. One of them picked herself up and put out a little hand as if saying, *I'm all right*. Her mother sat back down, waving. The boy ran to his mother, wailing the whole time, and only stopped when he was in her arms. I could hear her soothing him, and his theatrical sobs; maybe he just wanted to be there a moment longer than strictly necessary.

That made me smile, and I continued stretching my muscles as I breathed in the scent of the grass all around me enjoying the feel of the sun on the back of my head.

I need to meet her.

It came out of nowhere. The thought practically slapped me in the face, but I nodded to myself. It's what I had been waiting for. Some kind of definitive answer one way or the other, and I finally felt settled about it. Maybe it was watching the kids play with their parents, I wasn't sure. All I knew was that I needed to meet her, even if it was a total disaster. Even if it didn't go the way I hoped it would. At least I would have answers, and that was much more than I had right now.

I finished stretching and stood up. I tested my shins out by bouncing up and down lightly, and they felt much better. Hitching my bag farther up onto my shoulder, I picked up the pace. It was time for me to meet my birth mother; I just had to clear it with my parents first.

18

Later the following morning I called a "family meeting." That was just how things ran in my house. I sat on the living room couch across from my parents and it felt eerily like the night I got expelled.

For the third time, I cleared my throat.

"What's going on, Liv?" my dad asked warily. His arms were crossed, as if he expected bad news, and he looked like he had aged a few years since the last time we had sat here together. My mom looked nervous.

"It's nothing bad, guys," I began, and added in a rush, "I e-mailed Ali because I'd like to go and meet her."

I held my breath waiting for their reaction. They raised their eyebrows in surprise.

"Oh!" my dad exclaimed.

"What brought on this sudden curiosity?" my mom asked cautiously.

"I've been thinking about it for a long time," I admitted quietly.

"How long?" My dad's voice sounded suspicious.

"Not all that long, Dad." I couldn't help but notice the way he was tapping his foot. Was it nerves? Impatience? I wasn't sure.

"Is now really the best time for this, though, Liv? You've had a lot of change recently..." my mom's worried voice trailed off.

I wasn't sure if there would ever be a right time, and I knew if I didn't do this now I might never do it.

"Are you really prepared for this, Liv? This is coming out of nowhere." The worry lines on my dad's forehead seemed to grow deeper as he echoed my mom.

"I figure now is as good a time as any," I replied gently.

How could I tell him that this was hardly coming out of nowhere and that I had essentially thought of nothing else for the last year or so?

More silence while they processed then my mom said, "Well, you're sixteen, sweetheart. I knew this day would come eventually. It's why I kept the lines of communication open."

"Wait, who's going with you?" My dad was onto logistics already, skipping the feelings stage few men were good at. "Destin is nine hours away."

I hadn't quite thought of how I was going to break this part of the plan down for them, so I just rushed into it too. "Well, Mela is coming of course," I started. I hadn't technically asked her, but I figured she would.

"And?" My dad saw right through me as usual.

"And Nate... And Lucas," I finished.

"Nope! Absolutely not!" He stood up, but my mom patted his leg gently and convinced him to sit back down.

"Who's Lucas?" My mom attempted to hide the curiosity I could see burning behind her eyes.

"...He's Nate's best friend." I danced around the question. Lucas and I hadn't even talked about what we were yet.

"You're sixteen, you can't just drive across the state unsupervised." My dad threw a look of disbelief toward my mom.

"Your dad's right, Liv. I'm not so sure about this."

"Look, I know it's scary, but this is something I have to do."

My voice was steady and confident, as if I were the adult soothing children. They just wanted to protect me, but I wasn't a little girl anymore.

"Forget it, Liv!" My dad grumbled like a bear.

"Is this really about me going with boys, Dad?" I said calmly. "Would it make a difference if I stayed and hung out with them here? You know it wouldn't. This is because you're afraid I'm going to get hurt. Right?"

He stared at me for a few moments. I saw his lip twitch down slightly and felt the familiar sting of tears.

"I just…I just think it's too much for you right now," he mumbled.

"Maybe. But that's life, isn't it? We don't always get to choose what gets thrown at us. Maybe I need to deal with the big stuff right now so that I can move on. Maybe it's better to get it over with now instead of wondering and waiting."

His mouth kept on turning down until it made a frown. After a few minutes of silence, he spoke again. "Here's the deal. You'll call twice a day and answer every text we send. If we call, you answer. Got it?"

"Of course, Dad," I agreed quietly.

"And you'll take maps with you. Don't just rely on GPS."

I gave him a small smile and nodded.

"And you need to be safe, honey," my mom threw in for good measure.

My voice was thick with emotion. "Thanks, guys."

I excused myself and quickly retreated to my room. Wasting no time, unwilling to try my own resolve, I sat down at my desk to type out another e-mail to Ali. I hit reply on the one she had sent me.

Hi Ali,

I talked with my parents and they are fine with me coming down to meet you. My best friend Mela will be coming with me as well as her boyfriend and his best friend. Is that okay with you? I'm not really sure when we should plan this for. Do you have any ideas?

Olivia

Why had I told her all that? Perhaps because I wanted her to know I had people, that I was coming with a *contingent,* and not alone; not alone, like a beggar?

Don't be absurd, Liv.

In logistics mode like my dad, I figured that if we all pooled our resources, we could probably afford a couple of cheap hotel rooms and the gas to get down there. We might not eat anything but cheap sandwiches for a couple of days, but we'd survive.

Now that it was actually going to happen, I was starting to feel really anxious. I knew Lucas was waiting to hear how it had gone with my parents, so I sent him a quick text before heading to work for my shift.

> Hey, you. My parents are ok with the trip. I'll fill you in later.

There was a gentle knock on the door. I went to open it and found my dad standing there. I hoped he hadn't changed his mind.

"Here," he said gruffly and shoved something into my hand. I looked down and was shocked to see a stack of cash.

"Dad!" I started to protest.

"This is for gas and food. Your friends shouldn't have to pay for it. And get a hotel room for you and *Mela*. This isn't for partying or anything else, okay?" He pulled me into a bear hug before I could answer. I breathed in his familiar aftershave and blinked back the tears that threatened to spill over.

"Thanks, Dad," I whispered into his chest.

At Brew I greeted Sara with a small smile, and then I kept myself busy by cleaning the countertops, scrubbing the toilets until they glimmered, and shining the cutlery.

"Are you sure you're only sixteen?" Sara asked with a laugh at the end of my shift.

I laughed back. "Yeah, pretty sure."

"See you next shift!" she called after me as I left.

I was jingling my car keys in my hand in the parking lot and accidentally dropped them. As I bent over to pick them up, I noticed movement out of the corner of my eye. My blood ran cold: this time Chris *was* standing just a few feet away from me. He took a step toward me and I backed away. I hadn't seen him since the night he attacked me. He tilted his head questioningly.

"What's the matter, Liv?" he asked innocently.

"Stay away from me." I wished my voice hadn't shaken.

His eyebrows creased with frustration as he took another step in my direction and I took a step closer to my car, keeping him in my sights at all times. His eyes narrowed. My breathing started to quicken, and I could feel that panic was setting in.

"I'm not here to hurt you," he said gently. As gently as a cobra.

He stepped forward, I stepped back.

"How did you know where I was?" I tried to sound confident, but again my voice broke at the end.

"This is a really nice place, Liv. The lighting here makes it the easiest place for me to see you. I've been waiting for the right time to say hello."

The realization that he'd been watching me made me sick, even as he slid closer. How long had he been doing that? Was it just here, or had he been following me around without me realizing it? That had been him, then, watching me at the track? My hands were shaking uncontrollably.

"Stay the hell away from me!" I cried out.

"Don't be like that, Olivia." He raised a palm as if to keep me there. "This was all a misunderstanding. After all the time we spent together, don't tell me that it was easy for you to let go. Don't tell me that you haven't missed me as much as I've missed you."

He reached for my hand and I yanked it away, slamming it into my car door. I didn't even register the pain I ought to have felt. How could I have been so stupid? I was so distracted by everything else these last few weeks that I had forgotten to be on guard about him. The parking lot was deserted, but I could see Sara chatting with a regular inside.

"I have nothing to say to you, so just leave me alone."

I kicked myself internally for not sounding braver.

"See, that's the thing. You also had nothing to say to the police about that night, and that's how I know you still want to be with me. It's not easy for me to admit my feelings. Why don't you stop playing these games and let us work things out?"

Chris was so close now that I could smell the alcohol on his breath. I swallowed my fear and stood as tall as I could. Timidity was not my friend right now.

"You're right, Chris," I said slowly.

His eyebrows rose in surprise as a smile began to spread across his face.

"The lighting *is* great around here. That's why my boss is looking at us, and why she's probably asking that regular to come out and see if I'm okay." I turned my chin up defiantly.

Immediately his smile faded, and he whipped his head to the side to see that Sara was in fact staring at us. He didn't need to know that we couldn't actually see much from inside. I stood there praying that he'd believe my bluff, all the while inching my hand closer to the handle of my car door.

"Let's finish this chat another time, then, shall we?" he murmured too close to my ear as I flinched away from him.

"No, thanks." I spat the words at him as I opened my car door with determination.

"Just a misunderstanding, Liv. You can't avoid me forever..." He laughed lightly and let the words linger as he backed away.

Quickly, I got into my car, slammed the door shut, and locked it. My right hand had begun to hurt so badly that it took me three tries to get the keys in the ignition. I put the car in drive and floored it out of the parking lot, frantically turning to make sure Chris wasn't following me. Tears streamed down my face, as if I were melting down after holding steady during the terror.

I held the steering wheel with my left hand and put the right one under my armpit, as if that could make it better. All I could hear was my muffler and a shushing sound I couldn't identify as I sped down the street. I suddenly realized that it was coming from me.

Shhhh, shhhhh, shhhhh. Was I trying to calm myself down? I wasn't sure. *You've gotta breathe, Liv,* I told myself firmly. When I did, the air felt foreign in my lungs. I kept glancing in the rear-view mirror at the dark road behind me.

Turning down Nate's street, I formulated a plan as I pulled up to his place. We were leaving for Destin tonight.

19

The sun was coming up over the horizon. I watched as the sky turned from bright red to orange to a beautiful buttery yellow. My head rested against the car window as we began driving out of the city. We were just passing Banting when Mela's sleepy voice broke through my thoughts.

"Isn't that Chris's car?" she mumbled.

"What? Where?" I demanded, jumping up.

She pointed to the empty parking lot across the street from the school. Sure enough, his black Camaro was parked in the middle of the lot, and I could just make him out in the driver's seat.

"What a freak that guy is. Just as douchy as his ugly car," she muttered, much more awake than she had been a minute ago.

"Who's Chris?" Lucas asked.

"No one," I said almost too quickly as I absentmindedly rubbed my aching hand. Mela shot me a look but kept quiet.

"I love a surprise road trip as much as anyone, but can we please get some coffee up in here?" she begged Nate.

"We just left, Mel, can't you wait a bit?" I glanced back nervously in the direction of Chris's car, even though we had left it way behind.

"You want me to wait? For caffeine?" She turned in her seat to look at me.

I shrugged in defeat and she snickered. I hadn't slept at all, and I needed some caffeine as well, I just wanted to put more distance between us and Chris. Why was he waiting in that parking lot? For me to show up at school?

I almost jumped again when Lucas unfolded a blanket over me. *He must think I'm cold instead of distressed.* I tried to pull it farther up my lap but winced from the pain in my hand. I could feel him watching me, so I patted the blanket, as if it was where I wanted it to be.

Nate pulled up to a coffee shop and jumped out with Lucas to get our drinks. As soon as they were out of earshot, Mela turned to look back at me.

"Remind me again why we had to do this today instead of waiting?" she asked suspiciously.

I cleared my throat. "It was just something I needed to do now. I didn't want to chicken out." I kept my eyes focused outside, at the passing cars.

"Liv, what happened last night? I haven't seen you that freaked out since the night Chris—" The look on my face made her stop in her tracks. She let out a slight gasp. "Liv, did he—?"

I shook my head. I wasn't ready to even think about it. We sat in silence until the guys came back to the truck, but the way she was shifting in her seat told me I hadn't heard the last of it.

The traffic was beginning to pick up, and with fresh coffees in hand, we got onto the highway and headed west. I sipped my coffee for so long that it was ice cold by the time I finished it. Mela kept us on course with the maps I had grabbed from my car before we left. She found the novelty of them so charming that she refused to use the GPS. We eventually pulled up to a much nicer hotel than I would have been able to afford without the money my dad forced me to take. I felt a sudden surge of emotion toward my parents and smiled to myself.

"What are you smiling about?" Lucas asked me.

"Just…my dad."

We got adjoining rooms thanks to Nate's credit card. Mela and I settled into our room while they went to theirs. I lay on the bed with my arms over my eyes. Maybe I could just sleep for a while, before having to deal with anything.

Mela's quiet voice broke the silence. "Are you nervous?"

She was sitting on the edge of her bed facing me, her dark curls cascading down her back. I sat up slowly and crossed my legs.

"Yeah, I am. Ali doesn't even know we're in town yet."

"What??" Mela cried with a disbelieving laugh.

There was a knock at the adjoining door, and she went to unlock it. Lucas popped his head into our room.

"Hey, do you want to come for a walk with me?"

Mela smiled encouragingly at me and squeezed my shoulder as I walked by. I followed Lucas down to the elevator in silence. Once we were outside, we headed to the water since we could see it from our rooms. He tried to slide his hand into mine, but I gasped from the pain.

"What happened to your hand, Liv?" he asked in a low voice. I looked away as I answered him.

"I smashed it against my car last night." I hoped he would drop it. We walked down a path along the beach.

"What aren't you telling me?" he asked quietly.

"What do you want me to say, Lucas?" I tried to feign innocence, but I didn't even sound convincing to myself.

He didn't look at me, but instead said seriously, as if he were two or three times his age, "I want you to tell me what happened to your hand because I think it has to do with that Chris guy. What's your history with him, Liv? The way Mela talks about him makes me think he hurt you somehow."

I was good at hiding things, but he was more intuitive than I'd realized. I took a seat on a bench facing the water, and he wordlessly sat next to me. I let a few moments pass before I spoke.

"We had been dating for a few months before it happened."

As I told him about the night Chris attacked me, I felt him stiffen beside me. The sound of his belt buckle undoing, the way my tears had tasted as they poured into my mouth, my muffled screams, all of it played through my head and once again my hands started to shake. When I finished, Lucas seemed frozen beside me.

"What happened last night?" he asked eventually.

"He showed up after work and was waiting for me by my car. He had been drinking and kept saying how it was all a misunderstanding, and that he missed me and wanted to work things out." I cringed as I said it. The thought of being anywhere near him made me want to vomit.

Lucas stood up suddenly and started pacing back and forth, muttering to himself. Nothing he said made any sense to me. His fists kept clenching and unclenching and perhaps he saw the alarm in my face, as he stormed away and kicked sand into the air angrily.

From a distance, he turned to say, "I hate the thought of anyone hurting—" He threw me a look and went on. "Any guy that hurts a girl…it drives me nuts. Maybe it's good he's not here so I can't kill him."

What Mela had told me about that day with his mom made me realize this must be a real trigger for him. How long had he been witnessing men hurt his mother? It made me sad to think about.

Nevertheless, I said, "Can we just deal with what's in front of us for today? I can't process Chris *and* meeting my birth mother at the same time."

He still looked like he wanted to protest, but after a moment, he lowered his head and said, "Yeah, of course. Let's do that." He gave me a smile, but it didn't reach his eyes.

We headed back to the hotel, and I managed to get some privacy to call Ali. I dialed the number with uncertain fingers and held my breath as I waited for her to pick up.

"Hello?"

At the sound of a woman's voice, I nearly panicked and hung up.

"Ali?" I cleared my throat.

"Yes?" she sounded suspicious. She probably thought I was a telemarketer calling to offer her duct cleaning services.

"It's Olivia."

There was a pause on the other end.

"Hi!" She masked her surprise with an exclamation. I could almost see the mark coming out of the phone, floating in the air.

The pit of my stomach felt rock hard. "Hi, sorry to call you like this." Why was I apologizing? I wasn't sure, but it felt like I should.

"Oh, you're fine. What's up?" Her voice wasn't familiar the way I thought it would be. She sounded like a stranger.

"My friends and I are actually in town right now." I sounded so quiet, I wondered if she could even hear me.

"In *Destin*?" Her voice rose by a few octaves.

"Umm, yeah." I grimaced.

"Do I even want to know how this happened?" she said with a quick laugh. The sound made me smile.

"It kind of just…happened." My face felt hot with the sudden shame of springing this on her.

"Well, at short notice like this, I guess my family won't be able to see you, but I can meet in a couple of hours."

I tried to match her lightness. "Okay, sure. That sounds great."

She told me where to meet her, and I wrote it down. That simple.

"See you then, Olivia."

"Sure. Bye…Ali." I cleared my throat again and looked up at the ceiling, wondering why I had to sound like an idiot for our first call.

As soon as I was off the phone, Mela burst through the adjoining door. Clearly, I hadn't been afforded quite the level of privacy I had asked for. "Were you listening with a glass on the wall?" I asked sharply. She didn't look put off, only eager to know the result of my call, so I said, "She can meet me soon."

"Alone?"

"Yeah." I forced a smile and excused myself to the washroom. I could hear the boys coming in and the three of them talking while I stared in the mirror at myself.

My family won't be able to see you. She had said.

My family, not yours.

I should stop. Maybe I was reading into this too much.

A tiny voice at the back of my mind whispered to me, *Or maybe you're reading the situation perfectly.*

20

Lucas drove me to the restaurant a couple of hours later. I hesitated to get out of the truck, and at the same time I almost wanted to hurry up and get it over with.

Would we instantly bond? What would it mean if we didn't?

"You'll be fine," Lucas said.

I had been so lost in my own thoughts that it didn't occur to me that time had passed and that he had been watching me. I nodded and hopped out of the truck. As I crossed the deserted parking lot, my eyes flew everywhere as if I were some sort of spy going into the enemy's den and figuring out all possible exits. The restaurant stood alone on a bend in the road, overlooking rocks and the sea. We were so near the water that I could feel the spray on my face.

Managing to overcome the desire to turn around and get more encouragement from Lucas, I instead pulled at the large wooden door. It was heavy and my grip was slippery, so I struggled for a moment. When I let go, stepping inside, it closed on me, pushing me forward.

Even the door expected me not to be a coward.

Everything about the restaurant felt vast: the large windows framing a tall lighthouse to the left, the deck that might fit thirty tables, the waves crashing below. The walls were pastel-colored and there was no artificial lighting. No need; the day invaded the place, showing me table linen that was spotless and vivid fresh flowers at every table. I suddenly wondered if I'd be able to afford anything in here.

A waitress came by and offered to seat me.

"I'm actually meeting someone."

"Then it's likely her because no one else seems to come here at this time." She laughed lightly and pointed at the only other person in the restaurant.

I knew it was her immediately since she looked exactly like her pictures. She was seated facing me but distracted by her phone, so I had time to look her over as I walked. Ali looked like a powerful CEO or some kind of well-off businesswoman. She was dressed to perfection in black dress slacks, jacket to match, and a crisp white blouse. Her ankles were crossed, showing off her classic black heels. The sun made her blonde hair gleam the way the sun sparkles on the water, and her eyebrows were creasing the way mine did whenever I concentrated. I practically tiptoed over to her table, feeling like I might run out of oxygen as my heart was hammering so wildly.

She had chosen a place right beside the water. I rounded the wooden table and she looked up as I approached her. A wide smile lit up her face as she stood up.

"Olivia, it's nice to meet you." Her voice was warm, and I smiled in return.

"It's nice to meet you too," I replied shyly.

Should we hug? The silent question hung awkwardly in the air as we faced each other. She was the one to step forward and place her arms around me rigidly. I barely had time to return the embrace before it was over. The sweet smell of her floral perfume lingered on me. I breathed it in deeply as I took my seat across from her.

As soon as I caught her eye, I looked away. It was like looking at a reflection, only my skin was darker than hers.

"So, welcome to Destin!" Her voice was confident and sure.

"Thank you." I sounded flat in comparison.

"We have a lot to talk about, don't we? Why don't we get the ordering out of the way first, and then we can relax and chat?"

She was obviously used to taking charge of situations, and that was fine with me. I looked down at the menu in front of me, but I could not have said what was on it. Once more, she came to the rescue, as if this whole thing had been scripted, but only she had had a look at the script.

"You should try one of their blueberry muffins. They are to die for," she suggested.

"I do love a good muffin." I managed to smile as I said it. "Unfortunately, though, blueberries seem to give me migraines for some reason."

"I get those too," she murmured.

"You do?"

"I do! My mother and grandmother get them as well. Must be some kind of family curse." She laughed.

Following her cue, of speaking so openly about family and seeming to include me, I asked, "Is there anything that can take the pain away? Because nothing I've done so far has had any impact." I waited with bated breath.

"I actually have a prescription I take that reduces the pain by about ninety percent. I can write it down for you if you want?" she offered.

"Yes!" She was hardly done speaking before my outburst.

Finally—and within minutes of meeting her. I had never discovered if the migraines were provoked by stress or some bad habit, and now I knew it was a genetic condition. She had already pulled a piece of paper and a pen out of her purse and jotted down the name of a medication, handing me the paper. Our fingers touched briefly. Her nails were perfectly manicured and mine were all different sizes since I hadn't bothered to trim them lately. I pulled my hands back in embarrassment and folded them on my lap, clinging to the paper she had given me. Her penmanship was beautiful.

The same waitress came by and took our orders. Sweet tea and a lemon muffin for me, coffee and a scone for Ali. I wondered if I should read into the fact that we were just ordering a snack instead of a meal, but I decided to let it go.

"Wow, you two really look alike!" The waitress' mouth popped open. Ali was simply smiling, so I relaxed. No one had ever said that to me about a family member before. I allowed myself to revel in the satisfaction for a moment. The waitress left to get our drinks and we sat in silence for a few moments.

"This is a nice place," I said.

"Yes, I come here often. The smell of the ocean, the way the birds soar through the air, the waves crashing against the rocks..." She sighed happily. "I know most people can't stand seagulls because they're so obnoxious, but I swear I must have been some kind of bird in another life. Nothing ties them down, they're so…free. Well, I must have been either a bird or a sailor anyway. Never having to leave the water sounds magnificent."

Clinging to her every word, I nodded in agreement. She sounded so sophisticated, it felt more like she was reading from a book than just chatting.

"What about you? What would you have been in another life?" she asked curiously.

Not given away. I was filled with shame at the thought, and could never have said it, but it was there. Instead, I said, "A lighthouse keeper." We both glanced at the lighthouse just beyond us.

"That seems like a lonely existence," she mused.

"I don't mind being alone. I think it's sort of beautiful the way they lead people back home safely. Or I'd be a mermaid. Living in the ocean, under it, is what sounds like a dream," I added.

Ali tilted her head back and laughed easily. I felt a smile slowly spread across my face.

"Tell me about yourself, Olivia," Ali prompted. "I mean, about what you really like to do."

"I write. I'm thinking of becoming an author someday," I confessed.

"That's wonderful! There are a lot of writers in my family."

"Migraines and writing, huh?" I was getting some mojo back.

At this, she let out another peal of laughter. I liked how her eyes crinkled at the corner without making her look wrinkled.

"Do your parents like that you want to do that? What are they like?"

"Tall," I said. "Honestly, I look like a child in comparison. They're also very loud whereas I'm much quieter." I wasn't sure why I was explaining it to her in comparisons, but she grew serious and nodded with understanding.

"How are your parents with this?" She pointed from me to her and back.

"They understand that it was something I had to do. My mom and I are close. I tell her nearly everything." I hoped it was okay that I called her my mom. Would that hurt Ali's feelings? She didn't seem to notice.

"*Nearly* everything?" she asked with a knowing laugh.

"Well, a girl's gotta have some secrets." I took a sip of the tea the waitress had left in front of me.

"What about your friends? They came all this way with you?"

"Yeah, Mela's been my best friend since we were toddlers. She's basically family, for all intents and purposes. Her boyfriend Nate drove us up in his truck, and his best friend Lucas came too." I stumbled on Lucas's name because it felt like a lie to call him Nate's best friend and not my boyfriend, although we still hadn't had that conversation.

"Lucas is *just* Nate's best friend?" Ali read between the lines well. I blushed and smiled as I looked down. I ran my thumb up and down over my mug feeling the single imperfection on the side.

"I like him, a lot actually. He makes me feel safe." It was foreign to confide in someone who looked like me. I liked it. Her eyes twinkled softly as she took a delicate bite of her scone.

"Can I ask you something?"

Her eyes registered fear for a split second, but she nodded for me to go on.

"What can you tell me about my birth father?" I asked nervously.

She cast down her eyes and sat farther back in her chair.

"It's just that I know nothing about him, and I've always wondered…" I trailed off.

Until now, the mistress of the situation, Ali seemed to collect herself before answering.

"There's not a whole lot I can tell you to be honest. It was a long time ago, you know? You're just sixteen and you look like a young woman, but that's not how I was." She cocked her head at me. "You remind me of him; you have his smile and the same twinkle in your eye. He and I met and it was a very intense time. We thought we were adults living the way we were. He was young and reckless; I was even younger and more careless. My mother was convinced he was on his way to jail." She stopped and smiled sadly.

"Did—did you keep in touch?"

"No." She shook her head, her face serious, as if to make sure I understood it had been impossible. "I never wanted to find out what happened to him; it was too heartbreaking." She stopped again and considered me for a long moment. Then she delivered a bomb: "He wanted to keep you. Even took me to court over it."

It felt as if my entire body had been electrified by some live wire.

"He wanted to keep me?" I could not get my voice above a whisper.

"At least he *thought* that's what he wanted." Shrugging, she went on, perhaps unable to read my horror and distress. "I realized that he was just a boy and I was just a girl. My father said he wouldn't help us, and it was so scary to think of doing it alone. Not to mention that he was struggling with his mental health, and I was frightened for and of him." Again she stopped, and her hand tapped the table in another gesture of finality. "It was an impossible situation. They convinced me that you would be better off with grownups who could take care of you and… they were right."

Leaning forward, she took a long drink of her coffee looking off to the sea. The sun now shone through a diamond on her finger, just above her wedding ring. It flashed, and even made a tiny rainbow. This clean, bright life in sun-drenched restaurants, her clean, bright hair and her flashing diamond were not what she would have had with my father—the dropout, the screw up, the crazy boy headed for jail.

A boy who had wanted me!

I sat frozen in the sun. *My father had wanted to keep me?* I didn't know that he had struggled with mental health. Did that mean I would as well?

Why would my grandparents refuse to help them? Hadn't I mattered to them? More questions burned inside me, but I stayed quiet.

"It took me a long time to get over what happened," she said. Her thumb pulled on her rings unconsciously as she added, "I eventually met my husband Mark, and now we have two beautiful daughters together: Leah who's twelve, and Erika who's thirteen. Even having a responsible husband by my side and being an adult myself, I saw what it was like to have a child, then two. I don't know how well I could have cared for you without help."

The pain in her eyes was unmistakable but it was accompanied by a determination that seemed misplaced to me—as if she were challenging me to contradict her, or even as if a tiny baby I might have been her enemy.

"Can you tell me about them?" I knew I shouldn't ask, but I also could not help it.

"Sure." Now her smile was fond. "Leah is the joker of the family. She always has everyone in stitches. Erika is more serious and very dedicated to her horseback-riding career."

Never had I thought of myself as a big sister, but letting myself float with her words, I thought about these two sisters I was going to get to know, and how much we might like each other.

"They sound wonderful. I've never had younger sisters before. It'll be nice to meet them someday."

Ali's eyebrows creased again, and she cleared her throat. Finally, she looked uncomfortable. "Olivia, they don't know about you." Her words once more had a finality to them that made my stomach queasy.

"Yet?" I asked hopefully, but I knew the answer.

She shook her head slowly. "It would just confuse them. I made a lot of mistakes in my youth, and I want to protect my daughters as much as I can. They can't have an older sister who's dating and driving across the state unsupervised. They'll think they can do the same thing at sixteen. I don't want them heading down the same path I did. I'm sure you understand."

Understand?

I understood only too well that she had just used the things I'd confided to her against me. Did she really think I was on my way to getting knocked up at sixteen? I shrank back in my seat and stared down at my hands. *My daughters, my family.* She was never going to tell anyone about me, was she? What was so wrong with me that she was ashamed of my existence?

"I don't know why I came here." I once again hated, really hated that I could not control my voice, and that it would break although I didn't want it to.

"I do," she said. "You needed closure. We both did. That's why I agreed to meet you. It's too late for us to be family, Olivia. You know that. I gave up that right the moment I signed the papers." Her voice was sympathetic yet firm. Her mind had been made up for sixteen years. This was just a courtesy meet up. A courtesy meet up in a deserted restaurant, with no chance of being seen together.

Why didn't she want to know me? Was I irreparably damaged? Was I so easily cast aside that she just figured she'd start over again and do it right the second time with her new family? Was I somehow...broken?

I was the daughter of the wrong boy, the one headed for jail or a mental hospital. I was the secret, the reject, the mistake.

She had rewritten the script, and I was the bit player that walked into a restaurant and then walked out.

My eyes filled with tears that I promptly forced back. I wouldn't give her the satisfaction of seeing me cry; she had taken enough from me. We sat in silence for several minutes, her fidgeting in her seat, me staring out the window.

"I see," I mumbled eventually.

"Did you have any other questions for me?" she prodded gently.

"No. I think I know all there is to know," I whispered.

Her chair scraped against the floor. A single tear rolled down my cheek as she gently squeezed my arm.

"I'm sorry that I couldn't be who you needed me to be."

She walked away like the determined businesswoman she appeared to be. She had just taken care of business. No hard feelings. She probably had appointments to get to, now that this unpleasantness was out of the way. The sound of her heels faded as I watched the waves crash against the lighthouse. I felt as though I were the rocks, getting slammed with wave after wave of emotion.

After a while, I sent a text to Lucas letting him know that I was finished and needed to be picked up. I stood up slowly and placed one foot in front of the other as I navigated through the restaurant without looking back.

The girl I was before meeting Ali stayed back at that table.

She was gone now. I had always known that I was adopted but this—this changed everything. I hadn't realized until now that I wasn't just adopted: I was unwanted too.

21

As I stood outside the restaurant waiting for Lucas to arrive, I leaned against a chain-link fence and kicked my foot back and forth in the gravel beneath my foot. Every time the waves slammed into the rocks I flinched.

Slam – *she never wanted you.*

Slam – *something is intrinsically wrong with you.*

Slam – *if your own mother doesn't want to know you, then no one ever will.*

I jumped as someone touched my shoulder.

"Sorry." Lucas's face was full of concern. "You didn't hear me pull up?"

I shook my head, pushed off from the fence, and moved toward the truck. Lucas fell into step beside me but stayed quiet. He seemed to know that I wasn't ready for words. We got into the truck and pulled out of the parking lot. As we drove along the highway, I could still smell her perfume on me. Her words replayed in my head.

It's too late for us to be family, Olivia. You know that.

I hadn't known that. But only an idiot would think that there was a chance of being grafted back into her biological family. I turned as far away from Lucas as I could while tears silently streamed down my face. *How could I have been so stupid? How could I have believed that meeting her would somehow complete me?* Instead, I was more torn apart than ever.

The smell of her perfume seemed to get stronger until it felt like I was choking on it.

"Can you stop the truck?" I asked Lucas.

"Uh, sure. Here?"

He sounded confused. I nodded and he pulled off to the side of the road. I immediately jumped out, leaving the door wide open as I bent over with my hands on my knees. I took some deep breaths to get the scent out of my nose, but nothing was working. *It must be on my clothes.*

We were parked on the side of a large, grassy field and just beyond it was the water. I straightened my back and began walking toward the ocean.

"Liv!" Lucas's voice was alarmed as he closed the truck doors and chased after me.

"What are you doing?" He grabbed my arm lightly, but I jerked it away.

There was only one way to get rid of the perfume. I strode through the sand and walked straight into the water fully dressed.

"Liv!" Lucas was calling my name from the beach, but I kept sloshing through the water until I was up to my neck in it. My jeans and long-sleeve shirt clung to me, and my shoes got heavy and made it hard to walk, but I continued anyway.

A wave was coming, and I faced it head-on, letting it slap me square in the face. Once beyond it, I turned and leaned back into the water, letting myself float. I stared up at the seagulls flying to and fro, and they reminded me of Ali's words. *Nothing ties them down, they're so free.*

Maybe you just want to fly away, Ali. Maybe your life isn't quite as perfect as you make it out to be. Not that I have a right to care, we're not family after all. I'm nothing to you.

I watched as a cloud drifted through the sky and transformed before my eyes. It almost looked like a mountain. I wondered if I could touch it if I reached high enough.

The waves bobbed me up and down as I continued watching the sky. With every bob, I sank just a little farther below the surface. It seemed almost too easy to just let myself sink. I floated peacefully to the bottom and lay down. Grabbing a fistful of sand, I released it, enjoying the way it shimmered in the water like a thousand diamonds. The salt burned my eyes, but I kept them open anyway. How long would it take to fall asleep down here? My lungs begged for air, but I liked it there.

I'm sorry that I couldn't be who you needed me to be.

Her final words to me replayed in my mind as everything began to go dark.

You're a mistake.

My chest started to jerk as I refused to give it oxygen.

You were never wanted.

I closed my eyes for just a second and released the rest of the air in my lungs. The sun shining above the water was what made me panic. *What the hell am I doing?*

There was so much water above me! Would I make it? I kicked off from the ocean floor and fought my way back to the surface. I gasped for air, sputtering and coughing, as Lucas's arms came out of nowhere and lifted me high enough above the water so that I could breathe deeply.

Still gasping, I found him standing beside me in the ocean, fully dressed as well, and I burst into tears. He lifted me up as I sobbed into his shoulder and he walked us out of the water wordlessly. His arm continued supporting me as we sloshed and squelched our way back to the truck. It was slow work since we were both wearing jeans.

By the time we got to the truck, we were both out of breath from the sheer effort of dragging our soaking selves through the sand. I caught our reflection in the truck window and started to giggle. We looked, in a word, pathetic. Lucas's eyebrows rose, which made me laugh even harder, and then he was laughing right along with me.

When I started shivering, he helped me up into my seat, got around to his, and started the truck while blasting the heat.

"Do you want to talk about it?" he asked quietly.

"There isn't much to say. She was clear—she has her family, and I'm not it."

"Liv—"

"The door's closed, it is what it is." I sounded mature, but not quite without bitterness, much as I tried. "I was looking for answers, and I got them. Maybe I was searching for them in the wrong place. The craziest thing she said is that my father, the screw-up, the one heading for jail, *he* wanted to keep me. And maybe he wasn't even responsible enough to know what that entailed, but it means a lot to me that he wanted me."

"Maybe the door to your mother is closed," he pondered aloud, "but it sounds like perhaps another door has opened?"

"Maybe. I don't really want to talk about it anymore, though, if that's okay? I wasn't trying to kill myself, just so you know."

He threw a nervous glance in my direction. "Okay."

"How did it go?" Mela asked as soon as we walked through the door of our hotel room.

I saw Lucas shake his head out of the corner of my eye and Mela's eyes widen at our dripping clothes. Leaving wet footprints in the carpet, I grabbed some pajamas from my bag, and went into the bathroom to shower. It wasn't easy taking off sopping wet jeans, but I managed eventually. I stood in the hot water until I finally felt thawed out.

As I put my hair up in a towel and hung my clothing in the shower, I carefully avoided looking at myself in the mirror. I didn't want to see the deadened expression I could feel stuck on my face. The patterned tile was cold beneath my feet and brought on a new wave of shivering.

By the time I stepped out of the bathroom, Lucas was gone and Mela was sitting on her bed, playing on her phone. My feet sank into the carpet as I headed to my bed, reminding me of the feel of the sand beneath my feet. It was unsettling. I got under the covers and lay down facing the wall.

Mela's bed creaked, mine moved and then she was next to me. She rubbed my back softly and just held me, knowing that I didn't want to talk. It was comforting, but then just as quickly I felt the pang in my stomach, telling me things weren't the same anymore.

"We'll go back home tomorrow," Mela whispered.

I thought I was *coming* home I thought sadly.

Maybe things will be better in the morning.

Or maybe this is your new normal.

I braced myself for whatever was to come.

22

We pulled up in front of Moorewood Park, where I had asked them to drop me off. I wasn't quite ready to see my parents, and I wanted to stretch my legs after driving all day.

Mela rolled down her window as I stood outside the truck.

"We'll drop your bag off at your place. Unless, of course, you want to haul it around with you?" She smirked.

"Nah, I'm good. Thanks."

Lucas pulled me into a long hug and kissed my lips. I paused for a few extra moments, hugging his waist.

"I'll see you later," he said.

I smiled up at him and stepped back as they drove off. A cobblestone path stood before me and weaved through the park; I stepped onto it and began my stroll. On either side of the path were beautiful orange and yellow milkweeds, and canna lilies with sunflowers strewn here and there. I watched the bees land on each flower, dust it with pollen and pause while they drank some nectar. They landed and took off so effortlessly that I felt myself lingering to watch them. They knew what they were doing; it was perfect.

The sound of children squealing with laughter filled the air, and I watched as some flew on the swings, while others kicked soccer balls back and forth in the field, and others did flips in the grass. I thought of my childhood, spent cartwheeling through every day.

A small dark-haired girl came running up to me on the path, nearly tripping in her enthusiasm. She looked no older than four or five and as she approached, I saw that she was holding a sunflower in her hand that matched the blue and yellow sundress she had on. She stopped in front of me and offered me the flower.

"Here you go, wady." Her singsong voice brought a smile to my face as I took the flower and thanked her. She beamed and continued running. I passed her parents on the path, smiling at them.

"Kayla, be careful!" her mother called loudly. I heard a thwap and the instant wailing that typically accompanies such a sound, and turned to watch her father scoop her up in his arms and kiss her injured hands until she shrieked with laughter and wriggled away to continue running and playing.

It reminded me of my parents, and I instantly felt the ever-familiar twinge of guilt. They had always been so good to me. They had chosen me and continued to choose me again and again, and here I was, looking for my worth in strangers.

If I was chosen, I could always be un-chosen.

I sat on a bench overlooking the park and ran my fingers over the uneven wood, attempting to stuff down the thoughts bubbling up to the surface. *Chosen.* That word felt like Pandora's box. Being chosen implied expectations the way being picked first for a sports team came with the assumption that you would deliver a win. *What if they had chosen wrong?*

I watched a little blond boy on the swing begging his mom to push him higher and higher. Up he went, straight into the sky, and then just as quickly down he came, hurtling toward the ground.

As he went up, I thought about the ways my parents had always been there for me. Kissed every boo-boo, wiped every tear, cultivated my love of literature by reading me stories every night.

As he came back down, I thought about the longing that never went away despite my attempts to ignore it. I longed for *my* people, the ones who looked like me, the ones who shared my DNA, the ones who were supposed to love and accept me simply for existing.

Back up he went, and I thought about the sacrifices my parents had made to raise four kids instead of just three. The long hours at work, scraping meals together, the worries they might never had had if they hadn't taken me in—and yet they never complained or made me feel *less than*, the way Ali had in a single conversation.

Down the boy went zooming toward the ground, and I was painfully aware of the emptiness inside of me. The hole that would never be filled by anyone but the ones I came from. I yearned to be welcomed by these strangers in a way I couldn't put into words. It was ingrained into my very cells, and not something I could just ignore anymore.

I watched a couple walking with their toddler and swinging her up into the air and back down again. She screeched with delight and begged to go higher each time. I remembered the rush of excitement I had felt as my parents did the same thing when I was a child. I agonized over whether or not they felt betrayed by my desire to search for my roots. Did they worry that it would reflect poorly on them? Would they assume I didn't want to be a part of their family if I continued searching for my biological one?

The wrinkles on my forehead deepened as I wrapped my arms around my chest trying to hold myself together. How could I feel so divided? I loved my adoptive family and was so grateful to be a part of their world. At the same time, I grieved for the family I was meant to have but didn't. I now had the choice to look for my birth father, who might be a good person or might be rotting in jail—or worse. What kind of choice was that?

I swallowed hard and stood up. Maybe it was time for me to go home. I didn't figure I was going to get any closer to answers out here in the park. I shuffled my feet on the cobblestone path, the ground uneven beneath me. I was still holding the sunflower Kayla had given me and threw her parents a wave when I walked past them. She eagerly sent her arms flapping so wildly, I thought they might fall off.

As I looked up the path, I was surprised to see my parents walking in my direction. They hadn't seen me yet and were strolling side by side with their fingers interlocked. I swelled with affection toward them and picked up my pace.

When I reached them, they didn't seem surprised to see me. Mela must have told them where I was. I flung myself into their outstretched arms right there on the path. They closed their arms around me, and I breathed in the familiar scent of Old Spice and hand soap from each. I shut my eyes and leaned my face into the space between them the way I always had as a child.

Love always protects, always trusts, always hopes, always perseveres.

I hadn't heard those words since I was a kid in Sunday school, but they came back to me suddenly, in the arms of the only parents I'd ever really known.

Love always protects.

They had always protected me. I knew they wouldn't be able to shield me from every heartbreak, but I was confident that they would try. And at that moment, that knowledge was enough for me.

23

My eyes were burning from staring at my phone for so long. It was challenging to look at it while simultaneously pretending to do my schoolwork. LA kept giving me sideways glances and I knew she knew that I was on my phone, but she was letting it slide.

I stared at Ali's smiling profile picture again as I scrolled through her posts. I was torturing myself, but I couldn't seem to stop.

So proud of my daughters this Mother's Day. I have the two best!

The words taunted me as I stared at the picture of Ali laughing with her girls. It looked like a picture from a professional photo shoot. They were all wearing white shirts with gray skirts. One of her daughters had dark brown hair and the other lighter hair that matched her mother's. *My* mother's... Whatever. I pictured myself in the photo. laughing along with them. but shook my head at the ridiculousness of it. *Like a ghost, Liv? Really?* I had been scrolling for so long that I had scrolled all the way back to May. I kept trying to picture myself with her in every photo, and I was going nuts.

I noticed that she had tagged both my sisters in one of the pictures, which sent me down an entirely new rabbit hole of creeping on them. Erika's feed was full of pictures of herself on horses. She was obviously excellent at what she did. She looked so self-assured, the way I imagined I might have been had Ali kept me. There were tons of pictures of her standing on podiums with medals around her neck and ribbons on display in her room. I wondered if that would have been my room, had Ali kept me, and dismissed the thought as quickly as it entered my brain. *Stop living in a fantasy, she was never going to keep you.*

"Olivia, could you at least *pretend* to be doing something productive?" LA's voice rang through the room and I shrank down in my seat. Guess she had lost her patience.

"Sorry," I mumbled.

I put my phone down and continued working on the activity she had prepared for us. I was supposed to be making a list of everything I ever wanted to accomplish, even if seemed ridiculous or unachievable. So far, I had written:

Author

The rest of my page was blank.

Making sure that she was back to working on her computer, I turned my phone back on. I hadn't stalked Leah yet, and since I was already in this deep, I might as well keep going—even if it *was* bordering on obsessive.

Leah's page was different. It was full of laughter and joy. There were pictures of her and her friends laughing, making ridiculous faces, blowing out candles on birthday cakes. There were documentary-type videos of her narrating her way through life. There were a lot of pictures of the ocean: in some she was in it, in others just a sun sparkling over the water.

Looking through her page reminded me of…me. It was weird to think that this stranger and I shared the same blood, and at least some of the same interests. I wanted to know her. It seemed so unfair that I couldn't. I thought about just messaging her anyway, but how could I do that when Ali had specifically said she didn't want them knowing about me? Maybe someday she would change her mind, but that could never happen if I went against her direct wishes.

Again I put my phone away and continued working on my list. Or rather, staring at it. What else did I want to accomplish? I ran my fingers through my hair and crossed my legs.

"You got ants in your pants or something today?" Cara inquired with a laugh.

"I know, I know. Sorry." I was back to my chronic apologizing as well.

Her sheet was nearly full. I shrank in my seat a little bit more. Was I really the only one who had no aspirations for the future? *Think, Liv, think.*

"What kind of author do you want to be?" I jumped in my seat, not realizing that LA was directly behind me and peering over my shoulder.

"Umm, a good one?" My cheeks were getting hot with embarrassment. *Just add the tears and the breaking voice, Liv, go ahead.*

She crouched down beside me. "Well, obviously. But what will you write about? Do you want to be on the New York Times Best Sellers List? Get specific, Olivia. Nothing becomes dynamic until it becomes specific." She stood back up, patted my shoulder lightly, and continued walking around the room.

I looked down at my sheet and scribbled

New York Times Best Selling author

on it. She was right, I used to have so many goals as a kid. Where had they gone? By the end of class, I had added a few more items and felt a bit better.

~~Author~~

New York Times Best Selling Author
Track & Field Olympian
Olympic Coach for track
Photographer
Happy & whole

Maybe on purpose, I was the last one ready to leave. As I stood up to go, LA called me over to her desk. I walked over slowly and stood in front of her.

"You okay? You disappeared this week." Her eyes showed true concern.

"Yeah, sorry about that. I had something I needed to do."

She gazed at me for a few seconds before speaking again. "How'd you make out with your list?" She nodded at the sheet of paper in my hand.

"Better. I added a few more things to it."

"There's something special about you, Olivia. I can't quite put my finger on it, but I have a feeling you're going to do amazing things with your life."

I stared at her, wide eyed. "You think so?"

"I do. And I don't say that to just anyone. I felt like you needed to hear it today." She smiled up at me and I looked down at the ground bashfully.

"Thanks," I mumbled awkwardly.

"See you tomorrow."

I smiled as I left. No one had ever spoken to me quite like that. Lucas was waiting for me just outside the door.

"Hey, you!" he said as he put his arm around my shoulder.

I leaned into him as we walked. "Hey yourself."

"Still stalking Ali?" he asked casually.

"Maybe." I grimaced and gave him a playful shove. "I found my half-sisters' accounts. Leah reminds me of myself."

"That's great. Do you think you'll reach out to her?"

The corners of my mouth drooped as I shrugged. "I don't

think so. Ali made it pretty clear that she didn't want that happening."

"Yeah, but what's she gonna do? Disown you? That ship has sailed." He sounded bitter.

I looked at him with surprise, then said, "I guess you're right. But still, I have a feeling that would start a war I'm not prepared to fight right now."

Secretly, I was holding out hope that she'd want to know me someday. It seemed too pathetic to admit out loud, so I kept it to myself.

"Fair enough."

"What are you doing now? Do you want to hang out?" I asked when we got to my car and he leaned against it. I didn't have to be at Brew for a few more hours.

"I would love to, but I can't. My mom wants to see me." The look on his face indicated that he'd rather be doing anything else.

"What for?" I blurted it out and then wished I could take it back. It was none of my business.

"I don't know, actually, but since it's the first time she's asked to talk to me in months I figure I should probably go." He pushed off from the car and kissed my lips.

"Do you want me to go with you?" I offered.

"Nah, that's okay. I'll spare you the family drama." He forced a laugh, but I could tell he was stressed. "I'll text you later."

I watched him walk away, and I wasn't sure why, but I felt unease growing in the pit of my stomach. When he pulled away, I waved, but he didn't see me, and my hand stayed frozen in the air for a few moments. I stared until I couldn't see the truck anymore.

Everything is gonna be fine, I told myself. I just wished that I believed it.

24

I was gripping the steering wheel so tightly that my knuckles were white as I saw Chris's Camaro waiting for me at Brew. *You have got to be kidding me.* I picked the spot closest to the door so that I wouldn't be anywhere near his car, but I had no idea how long he planned to wait there.

I stared at his car through my rear-view mirror and the fear that I had always felt at the thought of him was slowly turning to rage. *How dare he stalk me this way at work?* I toyed with the idea of calling the police on him, but what would I say? He's sitting in his car and I don't like it? They'd laugh me off the phone.

Still, when I got out of my car, I glared at him. Even though he was halfway across the parking lot, I could see him clear as day, just staring back at me. I inched toward the door, never turning my back to him—and my heart stopped for a full moment as he stepped out of his car. He leaned against it, lit a cigarette, and took a long drag. The smoke he exhaled hid his face for a moment, and I shuddered as if a rat had run over my foot and stepped into Brew.

My rage had given way to nervousness, and I was such a nervous wreck that Sara cut me off from serving anyone drinks when my hands shook so hard carrying someone's coffee that it spilled all over the counter. She put me on cash instead.

I fidgeted between swiping debit cards and shakily handing customers their change. More than one bizarre look got thrown my way as people moved away from the line.

I kept glancing out the window to see if Chris's car was still there; it was. If I squinted hard enough, I could just make out his silhouette in the front seat. Every few minutes I looked out at the parking lot, just to reassure myself that he was a safe distance from me.

A line had formed, and I got busy giving each customer their change.

I heard the next customer placing an order with Sara and my skin began to crawl. It was Chris. Our eyes met and he smiled while I instinctively stepped backward. He came forward and waited for me to ring him up. Now I stood my ground while I punched in his order, staring at his white hoodie and blue jeans rather than into his eyes.

"That'll be $3.42." I choked on every word.

He extended his arm toward me and I flinched before noticing the ten-dollar bill he was holding. My discomfort seemed to amuse him; his eyes crinkled with delight. I snatched the bill out of his hand and hurriedly grabbed his change. I held the money out and instead of taking it, he closed his hand around mine.

"Keep the change," he purred.

I jerked my hand away from his and sent the coins flying to the ground. His eyebrows rose as he smirked and took his drink. Much to my horror, he sat at the table closest to the cash register and slowly sipped his coffee while staring at me. No matter what I did to distract myself, I could feel his eyes on me.

"Do you want me to ask that guy to leave?" Sara whispered in my ear, making me jump. I didn't have to look over at Chris to know she was referring to him. Apparently, I wasn't the only one creeped out by him.

"Could you?" I asked.

I hoped that he would take a hint and leave the premises entirely, but I wasn't holding my breath. Sara walked over to his table, and though I couldn't hear what she was saying I saw his eyes darken. He shot an angry glance my way. His chair scraped loudly against the floor as he stood up and towered over Sara.

"Well, that's going to be a one-star review for this crap hole." He moved while narrating the review he was planning to write. "Was drinking my overpriced coffee when the manager decided to discriminate against me on the basis of my appearance…"

Sara hardly appeared fazed at all as she held out her arm and pointed to the door, directing him to leave the shop. He shot one more look my way and walked away slowly, as if he thought of himself as some sort of cool cowboy in a B-movie.

I exhaled what felt like a ton of air while nodding my thanks to Sara and continued to wipe the same spot on the counter I had been cleaning all shift.

"You might think about involving someone, even the police, to stop the stalking," Sara said in a firm voice. "He's been in here more than once, lingering like he was waiting for someone. Now I can see it's you he's been waiting for."

Should I call Lucas? I thought about what he had said on the beach in Destin: *Maybe it's good he's not here so I can't kill him.*

No, I didn't want to involve him in this. He would know how bothered I was. Chris had returned to his car; I held my breath, hoping that he would start the car and leave, but I wasn't that fortunate. It was just starting to get dark outside, and my mouth went dry as I realized that soon he'd be able to see in, and I wouldn't be able to see out. It was like some horrible scenario made up by a sick mind; in fact, it was—and the sick mind was his. I struggled to stay calm as my eyes darted between his car and the door.

Suddenly, out of nowhere, Lucas was marching straight across the parking lot, his eyes locked on Chris, whose eyes were still locked on me.

I rushed out the door, not minding the loud thud when I hit it, and ran directly to where Lucas was now dragging Chris from his car.

"You think you can prey on her?" Lucas yelled at Chris as he slammed him up against the Camaro.

"Lucas!" I hissed. I looked around as bystanders stopped to watch or approached.

"This my replacement?" Chris spat at me with a laugh.

"Don't talk to her. Ever." Lucas stepped between us and blocked my view. I tried to pull him back, but he shrugged me away and cracked his knuckles. Chris threw his head back and shook with laughter.

"Do you honestly think you can win a fight against me?" he jeered.

The muscles in the back of Lucas's neck were bulging, and he was practically vibrating. I had never seen him like this before. My eyes flew between the scene in front of me and the crowd gathering fast. *How can I stop this?*

"Lucas, come on, he's not worth it," I pleaded.

I didn't like the way people were surrounding us, like vultures waiting for carnage, but Lucas didn't seem to hear anything I was saying. One of his arms was held out in a protective stance in front of me and I watched as he shifted his weight from one foot to the other and back again.

"Just leave, Chris," I muttered through clenched teeth, peeking out from behind Lucas.

Chris scoffed in disbelief. "Me? I'll tell you what, Liv. I'll leave when you dump this trailer trash and agree to come back to me."

The last thing I saw was Chris waggling his eyebrows suggestively, right before Lucas's fist connected with his face.

25

Chris dropped to the ground like a sack of potatoes. He looked around stunned, as though he couldn't believe Lucas had that kind of strength.

"Big mista—" I gasped as Lucas kicked him in the ribs before he could finish speaking. Chris staggered to his feet, clutching his waist, and spat blood on the ground. Was it blood from his mouth or an internal injury? I didn't care about Chris, but about the trouble Lucas might be getting into for my sake.

Lucas was pacing back and forth with his fists clenched. Chris lunged at him, but Lucas ducked out of the way and landed another punch to the side of his head. He was like a cat dancing around Chris on the balls of his feet.

Too late we realized that Chris was closer to me than Lucas, as he grabbed my arm and tried to pull me toward his car.

"We need to talk," he snapped, apparently determined not to admit Lucas was beating him although his mouth was full of blood. I yanked my arm away from him just as Lucas pulled him back and threw him to the ground.

"Don't touch her!" Lucas roared.

He kicked Chris in the side several times and I flinched at every thud. He then launched himself on top of him and cracked him in the face. The sound of Chris's head slamming back against the pavement seemed to echo through the parking lot and wake up the audience.

Someone started screaming for Lucas to stop as he wound his arm back and punched Chris in the face again and again. Two guys pulled Lucas off and I watched Chris roll back and forth on the blood-splattered pavement, moaning. A girl was screaming, and as I looked around to identify her, Sara was suddenly in my face, shaking my shoulders.

"Olivia! Stop screaming!" she shouted at me.

Huh? I was the one screaming? I closed my mouth and the sound stopped. A woman beside me was on her phone.

"Yeah, the parking lot at Brew. He's hurt pretty bad, it looks like. I dunno, yeah, I'd send an ambulance..." I tuned her out and frantically searched for Lucas.

He was being restrained by the two guys who had pulled him off Chris.

"Lucas!" I croaked, barely recognizing my own voice. I ran over to him, flung my arms around his waist and pressed my head against his chest. The sound of sirens was growing louder; as they grew, so did my panic.

"Let him go!" I screamed as I shoved one of the guys holding his arms. *He can't go to jail over this, not for me.*

"Not gonna happen." The guy's voice was deep and gruff, and his face flashing red for some reason.

I whipped around to see the police car lights and two male officers approaching us on foot.

No, no, no, no! I screamed inside my head.

"I'm so sorry, Liv," Lucas whispered as one of the police officers turned him around and handcuffed his wrists behind his back.

"No!" I wailed and threw my hands on the cuffs, as if somehow I could make them disappear just by touching them.

"Step back, miss, or you'll be the next one in handcuffs." The arresting officer glared at me as I slowly stepped back and watched him put Lucas into the back of the police cruiser.

This isn't happening.

The harsh noise of wheels rolling across the pavement made me turn to see the paramedics loading Chris into the ambulance. I could barely make out his face with all the blood on it. One of his eyes was swollen shut. He still looked triumphant and he flashed me a smile through his cracked, bruised lips. I turned away so I wouldn't have to look at him.

My damned fingers trembled as I sent Mela a text.

Come to Brew. Lucas was arrested.

I put my phone back in my pocket and stepped across the parking lot at a snail's pace. Plopping down on the sidewalk, I put my head in my hands and closed my eyes. Behind my lids, I could see the look on Lucas's face as he battered Chris repeatedly. His eyes had been unfocused and empty as he swung his fist through the air.

Slowly, I realized that the parking lot was still full of activity. The remaining police officer was questioning the woman who had called 911. I cringed as she pointed directly at me and held my breath as he walked over to me.

"Miss? I'm officer Schmidt." He was tall and muscular, with a shaved head and piercing light blue eyes. "I need to ask you some questions about what happened here tonight." His voice was very official sounding.

"Me?" I stood somewhat shakily.

His thick eyebrows creased, and he gave me a knowing look. "What's your name?" His pen hovered over his notepad, waiting to record my answer.

"Olivia Jackson," I mumbled as he nodded and wrote it down.

"I was told you knew the victim and the assailant?" It didn't seem like a question.

"Yes, I know them." Assailant? Lucas wasn't a criminal, he was just protecting me.

"I'm going to need you to come down to the station."

"The station?" I crinkled my eyebrows as if I could not understand him.

"The police station, Miss Jackson." He spoke slowly, as though I was an idiot. "I can take you there in the police cruiser, or you can bring yourself. But you'll need to come now." He folded his arms across his chest.

"Now? I'm in the middle of my shift." I pointed helplessly to my apron with the word Brew written in cursive across the front. He leaned around me and looked in at the empty shop. Sara bustled behind the counter.

"Looks like they can spare you." The corner of his lip curled.

"Liv!"

Mela was running across the parking lot dragging Nate behind her.

"I'll expect you at the station within thirty minutes." He touched his finger to the top of his cap, turned, and walked back towards his car.

Nate and Mela walked up with wide eyes. It seemed like I had done nothing but surprise or worry them lately.

"What the hell is going on, Liv?" Mela demanded.

"I have to go to the police station and try to convince them not to press charges against Lucas for beating Chris to a pulp."

I said the words flatly and thought I was sitting back down on the sidewalk, but it was my legs giving way while my vision turned black.

26

I felt like I was floating. I tried to think of the last time I'd felt this light and couldn't. Maybe I had never felt this free before. It was nice not having anything weighing me down for once.

In the back of my mind, I knew that I was forgetting something really important, but I wanted to stay frozen in this place for as long as I could. A sudden flash of Ali's face interrupted my serenity. It disappeared just as quickly as it came. I settled back into the calm and thought of the day I met Lucas on the beach; it made me smile. The nagging feeling that something was off grew stronger, but I fought it. I knew I should try to open my eyes, and I didn't want to—not yet.

Out of nowhere, I remembered being underwater, clawing for the surface with my chest burning for air. I winced and pushed that thought out of my mind only for it to be replaced with the memory of Chris's body weight pinning me down.

I groaned and tried to sit up. Something heavy was on my chest, preventing me from moving. More unpleasant memories flashed through my head so quickly, it was as though I were watching a horror-movie reel of my life.

My eyes flew open to find Mela above me, shaking my shoulders roughly.

"Liv! Liv!"

How long had she been calling my name for?

"What happened?" I mumbled as I sat up, still on the sidewalk.

"You passed out!" She sounded alarmed.

"I did?" I looked around in confusion. Thankfully, no one besides Nate and Mela seemed to have noticed.

"Help me up, we've gotta get to the station."

I reached my arms up toward them, and almost began crying when I thought of Lucas, always reaching down to me with a smile, always pulling me up, up. They looked at each other and then back at me as they leaned down to help me.

"I'll drive." Nate ran his hands nervously through his hair and led the way to his truck. Mela kept her arm around my waist as we walked behind him.

"So, what happened? Lucas just showed up and started beating on Chris?" Mela wanted to know as I climbed into the truck and she clambered in after me.

"Sort of. Chris was sitting in the parking lot like the creep he is, just waiting. Then he came into Brew, got a coffee, and sat at a table staring at me until my boss made him leave." Mela's mouth opened with outrage at my words as I went on. "I was trying to decide what to do and how I was going to get out of there when Lucas showed up out of nowhere and dragged Chris out of his car."

"Holy crap!" Mela exclaimed.

"It was so weird. He didn't even come into the shop, he just went straight to Chris like he was on some kind of mission. I don't know what could have happened to set him off like that."

We both turned to Nate at the same time, realizing he probably knew what had happened but just hadn't thought to tell anyone yet.

Nate cleared his throat. "Maybe it's because of the fight he had at his mom's?"

"Well?" Mela demanded.

"I dropped him off at his place earlier because his mom asked to see him. I pulled out of the driveway but parked on the street because I was waiting for Mela to text me about what she wanted to do. I could hear Lucas yelling at someone, so I jumped out to see what was going on. I heard him say something like *you kept me from him all my life and I hope you're satisfied* or something like that? He stormed out of the house and I tried to stop him, but he just waved me off and muttered something about going to see you, Liv."

Dread was building in the pit of my stomach. What could have happened to make him so angry? He must have gotten there only to see Chris waiting for me.

Mela was chastising Nate. "How many times am I supposed to tell you that you need to communicate the important stuff?"

"It didn't seem that important. I mean, it's happened a few times..."

Mela lightly swatted his arm and shook her head. We pulled into the police station and my palms began to sweat.

"So, uhh, what's the plan here?" Mela asked.

"Storm in and demand they release him?" I threw my hands in the air helplessly.

Mela tilted her head to the side and gave me a look that suggested that may not be my best idea, but we got out and headed into the station anyway.

Inside a middle-aged woman sat at a desk behind a wall of plexiglass. Her hair was fiery red, she had on cheetah-print glasses with thick lenses and was chewing on a pen.

"Yes?" she demanded impatiently without looking up from her computer screen.

"I'm here to see officer Schmidt. He's expecting me." My voice was barely above a whisper. I had never been interrogated by a police officer before.

"Take a seat." She pointed to some chairs behind us and got on the phone. We had hardly managed to sit down before Officer Schmidt buzzed a door open.

"Miss Jackson, thank you for coming," he said rather pleasantly.

As if I had a choice…

"Please come with me." He motioned for me to follow him.

Mela and Nate threw me a double, encouraging smile. I stood up on wobbly legs and followed him through the large steel door. The sound of it closing made me feel like I was about to be thrown into a cell for the rest of my life. I searched around for Lucas but couldn't find him anywhere.

We walked down the hall and he led me into what I presumed was his office. Again he motioned, this time for me to take a seat while he rounded his desk and sat down on a rolling chair that had certainly seen better days. He struggled to pull himself closer to his desk as he picked up his notepad and a pen. I shifted uncomfortably in the cushioned seat across from him.

"So, Miss Jackson. You witnessed the altercation between Mr. O'Connell and Mr. Jamieson?" he began.

"Lucas and Chris? Yes."

"Who started the fight?" he asked.

"I don't know who started it," I said the words too quickly.

He raised his eyebrows as his pen hovered above the paper. "This will go a lot smoother if you're honest, Olivia." His voice was firm but kind.

"Officer Schmidt, I don't know what happened. Chris has been stalking me at work. My boss even had to ask him to leave tonight." Once again, I hated that my voice was shaking and that the pitch was much higher than usual.

"Why didn't you call the police?" he asked. The wrinkles in his forehead increased with doubt.

"I didn't know what to say," I admitted.

"Lucas is in a lot of trouble. Chris is at the hospital now and if he presses charges, which he has every right to do, then things won't be easy from here on out." He sounded sympathetic, which surprised me.

"Officer, anything Lucas did tonight was to protect me." As the words escaped my mouth, I realized that they were the truth. Lucas had been trying to keep me safe since we met.

"Why would he need to protect you? Has something else happened besides the stalking?" the officer prodded.

I took a deep breath. I hadn't ever planned to tell anyone what Chris had done, but if it would help Lucas get out of there, I had to try. I looked into Schmidt's kind blue eyes and told him everything. Afterward, he leaned back in his seat and pursed his lips.

"That's a heavy accusation," he said soberly.

Tears filled my eyes as I nodded. "It was the scariest moment of my life. Lucas is one of the good guys, officer. He would never hurt someone unprovoked."

"I believe you. But that doesn't change what happened tonight." He swiveled slightly in his bad chair. "Are you going to press charges against Chris?"

"Would it do anything to help Lucas?"

"Probably not. Unless you had witnesses to the event, it's not likely to go far and even if you did... Our justice system is broken, Olivia. We put the bad guys away only for them to be released on technicalities or given a slap on the wrist." He took his baseball cap off and dropped it onto his desk to rub his head in frustration.

And I sat back in defeat. *Great.*

"So you can't let him go?"

"No. We need to hear from Chris as to whether or not he's going to press charges, and then there will be a hearing."

Wiping the tears off my cheeks, I nodded. He leaned forward again, and opened and closed his mouth as though he were wrestling with himself.

"Look, I shouldn't be telling you this, but if you think there's any way you can convince Chris not to press charges, then we'd have to release Lucas. But if Chris is as dangerous as you say, you shouldn't be alone with him. He's at the hospital now, but that window is closing."

My eyes widened at his words. Convince Chris not to press charges? *How in the world was I going to do that?* He nodded slowly at me, then toward the door.

"Good luck, Olivia. Be safe."

27

"We're coming in with you. Don't even try to stop us."

We had been parked outside of the hospital for several minutes sitting in silence, and Mela was all up in arms.

And when she was up in arms, she could be formidable. She was mad at me for hiding things, and she was right—because she ended up involved in them anyway, for one. I was still trying to muster up the courage to face Chris. I was terrified that he would corner me even if he was lying in a hospital bed, and I could do with her help and Nate's.

I couldn't be a one-woman band anymore; in fact, I hadn't ever been one.

"Come, but stay outside of the door so that he'll talk," I said. I hoped I sounded as grateful as I felt. "I don't want him getting spooked by an audience."

She agreed. I pulled out my phone and made sure that it was ready to record. I had one shot to do this, and I knew I needed to make it count. I also knew Chris was no one's fool.

The closer we got to the door of the hospital, the dumber my plan seemed. Still, it was all I had. I walked straight over to the nurse's station and asked for his room, though I wasn't exactly sure if they would let me see him since I wasn't family.

"Are you Olivia Jackson?" the nurse asked.

"Yes," I responded. I couldn't believe it ... He had been expecting me.

"Room 3212 down the hall."

I trembled more with each step that took us closer to his room. The unnaturally bright fluorescent lights made me wince and I forced myself to focus on the tiled floor, counting each black and white square as we walked. Mela squeezed my hand, telling me she was there, but also telling me to get in kick-ass mode. Nate's hand was on my shoulder as he walked slightly behind us.

I had my guard with me.

Seventy-two squares later we arrived in front of room 3212. The door was closed. I took a deep breath and knocked softly.

"Come in," Chris called out.

As soon as I heard his voice, I had to resist the urge to run screaming from the hospital.

Mela and Nate nodded their encouragement once more. I had spent the last couple of months avoiding him at all costs, and now I was willingly walking into a room to be alone with him? What the hell was I doing?

You're saving Lucas.

Time to start the recording on my phone, which I did without trembling, for once. It was a mission; this was not only for me. I pushed the door open while my friends stayed out of sight.

I walked in and my breath caught as I looked at him. His face was badly bruised; he had two black eyes and a bloody scrape across his face that had matted his brown hair to his forehead. His right wrist was in a cast, so it was either fractured or broken, and he had gauze around his shirtless stomach.

Was it odd that I felt a sense of pride for Lucas rising in me? Probably. I didn't care.

"I knew you'd come, Olivia," Chris said quietly as he watched me from his bed. I shuddered internally at the sound of his voice and at the way he said my name. The bed rails were up, and he was sitting on top of the covers. The only illumination in the room came from the lamp on the wooden side table next to him, which cast an eerie glow on the room.

He really was the villain.

"Did you?" I asked. My voice did not shake.

"Mmhmm. I knew you'd need to make sure I was okay."

He was staring at me so intently that I took a step away from him. His eyes narrowed as he watched me. How was I going to convince him not to press charges if I couldn't even look at him?

"Are you? Okay?" I tried to sound compassionate, but I wasn't sure if he bought it.

"I'll be fine," he murmured. A long pause hung in the air before he went on. "Can I ask you something?"

"Yes," I braced myself for his question.

"Have you slept with him?" He winced even as the words came out of his mouth.

My jaw nearly dropped from shock, but I pulled myself together.

Where was he going with this? "No," I managed to say.

The relief on his face was instantaneous. "Good." He smiled and nodded to himself.

"Why would you ask me that, Chris?"

"I want to be your first." He actually looked and sounded shy.

Was he nuts or kidding? He couldn't be so delusional as to believe he still had a chance? But by the look on his face, I could tell that he was serious.

"I miss you, Olivia. I should never have let you go." He sounded so genuine that I was sure he believed his words.

"I have a very different version of events in my memory," I spat.

Chris grimaced at my words. "I am truly sorry for that, Olivia. I read the situation wrong. You know I'd never hurt you on purpose."

He waited for me to respond. And this was what I had been hoping for.

"So you finally admit to attacking me? To forcing yourself on me?" I demanded as I covertly tilted the phone just so in order to get him on video saying it.

"I just love you so much and wanted to be your first so badly that I lost myself for a minute."

He looked at me sorrowfully as I swallowed the acid coming up my throat.

"I won't press charges against Lucas if you agree not to see him again," he said. It was what he had been waiting to say. Even as he was being beaten, his focus had been on me. Love? More like an obsession. He didn't know how to love only how to possess. It was and would always be about him.

There he sat, playing the bruised martyr willing to suffer for a noble cause. *As if he thinks I'd fall for that.* I drew myself up.

"No," I said quietly.

His mouth flew open in disbelief, and his expression instantly changed to a much nastier one. "No?"

"You heard me."

"You'd rather be with that psycho?" he roared. I nearly laughed out loud and he saw it. I watched as he burned with anger, but I held my ground.

"I'll make your life a living hell, Liv. I'll press charges, and I'll keep showing up wherever you are—only you won't have him to protect you next time."

"I don't think you will, Chris," I said, almost dreamily.

"Oh, no?" he jeered.

"No. You see, I went ahead and recorded this entire conversation." I held up my phone. "I did that because I knew you'd threaten me. And now everyone will know the truth about you."

He lunged toward me, but his injuries had slowed him down, and the bars kept him from getting to the floor quickly enough. I backed up and handed my phone to Mela, who showed it to Chris while she wiggled her hips and finished by flipping him the bird. She disappeared. I could hear her and Nate going fast down the hall and laughing.

I hoped I'd caught everything, and I turned back to face him. His eyes burned with fury, but I was on a roll.

"The truth is that you're just a twenty-two-year-old coward who got your ass kicked by a kid five years younger than you *after* you tried to rape your sixteen-year-old girlfriend. Any way you look at it, you don't come out looking so hot."

"All that stuff could be interpreted some other way, thrown out—"

"By your daddy, huh? But you know who is going to love spreading the film around? The same Katie Bryan who spread lies about me. She doesn't much care who she targets, as long as the gossip is juicy. Not to mention this just being online on a loop. Crazy guy obsessing over his ex-girlfriend and blackmailing her after trying rape."

I took a step toward the door while he seethed.

"So here's what we're going to do, Chris. You're going to call the police station and tell them that you're not pressing charges against Lucas, or I'll send this video to everyone I know. I hear that you and my sister run in similar circles, so don't think this wouldn't get around to the people you know."

I watched him calmly as he clenched his fists on the bed. He looked livid. He looked like he needed the nurse.

"Do we have an understanding?" I finally asked.

He tilted his head to the side as though trying to determine if I was bluffing or not. I jutted my chin out and crossed my arms while he weighed his options.

"We have an understanding," he muttered.

My heart pounded so loudly I was sure he could hear it.

"I never want to see you again, Chris." I stared at him and waited for his acknowledgment.

A smile slowly lit up his face, which scared me more than anything else he had said or done up until now.

"All right, Liv. I won't come close to you since you have your blackmail," he began.

I turned my back on him as he went on.

"I'll just wait for you to understand how you really feel and come to me. I'll be more welcoming than you, of course. All will be forgiven."

The delusion wasn't worth a response. He could live the rest of his life in his fantasy, as long as he didn't come near me.

The way back through the hall was much shorter than the way in. Outside the hospital, Mela linked her arm in mine, and Nate trailed behind us, apparently happy to be the security detail.

The me from a few months before would have never found the courage to stand up to Chris that way. I smiled as I walked through the parking lot with my head held high. I had faced my fears more than once lately and lived to tell the tale.

Whatever doesn't kill us makes us stronger.

The girl who used to let people walk all over her seemed to be gone, and in her place was a new girl I hardly recognized. She was stronger, she was more determined, and she could do hard things. Maybe my future was still to be written, and by me.

28

I stood outside of the police precinct biting my lip and pacing back and forth. Nate and Mela had dropped me off and left the truck while they took her car back to his place. I had already called Officer Schmidt three times to make sure that Chris had dropped the charges.

"Yes, Olivia, he called. If you have him admitting to attacking you on video, are you sure you don't want to have him arrested?" I could hear his fatherly concern through the phone.

"I'm sure."

There was no way I would jeopardize Lucas's freedom by showing the recording to the police. Officer Schmidt himself had said that often guys got off with a slap to the wrist, and Chris's dad had money. While it made me feel furious that he might do this to someone else, I needed Lucas not to be punished for doing the right thing.

And it never hurt to have ammunition against a psychopath in your back pocket. I had made sure to send the recording to my e-mail and a copy to Mela. I wasn't taking any chances. I couldn't risk it being lost and us being right back where we started. At least he knew that I would join my proof to the chorus if anything ever came to light about him.

I stared into the large window overlooking the parking lot and caught the receptionist's eye again. She was still chewing on her pen, and I was just waiting for it to explode ink all over her face. Just when I was about to go back inside and demand an update, I caught sight of Lucas trailing behind Officer Schmidt. I breathed a sigh of relief as they shook hands and Lucas walked out the door.

I wasted no time. I immediately ran to him and jumped into his arms, squeezing his neck so tightly I thought I might choke him. He squeezed me back and laughed easily.

"Miss me?" he whispered as I slid back to the ground.

"Maybe a little."

"Me too." He leaned down and kissed my lips, and this time we stayed like that for a while.

Then I handed him the keys to the truck and pulled him toward it.

"Come on, let's go before they change their minds."

Officer Schmidt was looking at us through the window with a concerned look on his face. I turned back to Lucas and he lifted the corner of his mouth a little and gave a shrug.

"A man in prison gets hungry for his girl," he said. "The officer knows that."

We laughed as we drove, and I pulled his hand into my lap and held it tightly. I looked down at his hand and noticed the bruises on his knuckles. They seemed to be the only injured part of him, and I was grateful for that. The way he had come to my defense and protected me made me want to cry.

Something was nagging at me, though. What had Nate said he heard? *You kept me from him all my life and I hope you're satisfied,* or something like that?

"What happened tonight, Lucas?" I asked quietly.

He glanced at me. "Nate told you?"

I simply nodded. He watched the road as I felt his hand stiffen in my lap.

"My mom wanted to see me in order to talk about my dad."

"Your dad? You haven't seen him since you were three right?"

"Right. I guess he came to see me a few days ago, but she sent him away and told him I didn't want to have anything to do with him."

He probably knew I would understand, better than anyone, perhaps. *How dare she make that decision for him?* I squeezed his hand tightly in solidarity, careful to avoid his bruised knuckles.

"She waited until he had left town again to tell me, and now I have no idea how to get a hold of him." His voice broke on the last word and he cleared his throat to cover it up.

We sat in silence while he fought for composure. I looked out the window to give him some privacy.

"Anyway, I don't even know why I care so much. I was never sure if I even wanted to look for him. Having that decision stolen from me though…" he trailed off.

Adults taking our choices away, as if they had any right to. It had happened to both of us.

Lucas stopped the truck and I realized that we were at Pink Lake. I wondered if he had meant to drive there, or if his instincts had just taken over. We hopped out of the truck and I quickly slid my hand into his, partly to let him know I was there for him and partly because it was almost pitch-black outside.

We walked through the woods in silence as I racked my brain for something helpful to say, but nothing came to mind. Finding the rock we had perched on the first time we went there, he pulled me up the same way he had then.

"I'm sorry, Lucas," I whispered through the dark. I could see his face in the light from the fireflies.

"Me too."

I wrapped my arms around his waist and listened to his heartbeat.

"How did you convince him to drop the charges?" he asked after a moment. "I figured he'd be only too happy to see me rot in jail."

"Yeah, he would have. He threatened to have you locked up if I didn't agree to get back together with him." I smiled, though he couldn't see it. "Too bad for him I recorded the whole conversation and got him to admit to attacking me."

"Liv, that was dangerous! You shouldn't have done that."

"How could I not, Lucas? After everything you've done for me. The way you carried me when I couldn't stand. The way you made me feel wanted when—" My voice broke on the last word. *When my own mother didn't want me,* I finished in my head.

He pulled me closer and gave me a tight squeeze. "I've never felt this way about anyone before."

"Me neither," I whispered.

I wanted to stay in that moment forever, but I felt a pull even as I wrestled with myself. What had just happened to Lucas had brought the struggle to the surface: I still hadn't decided what to do about my birth father. I wanted to look for him, but all the what ifs were dancing inside my head.

What if he doesn't want me to find him?

What if he has a new family that doesn't know about me?

What if he rejects me the same way Ali did?

The last one made me wince.

"What are you thinking about?" Lucas asked.

"I can't decide if I'm going to look for my birth father or not," I admitted. "What your mother just did made me think about it again."

"Talk to me?"

It was just like him to offer to help me when his world had just been turned upside down.

"What if he's a total screw up? What if he is in jail? Or worse? What if he doesn't want me the way Ali didn't?" He knew the rest, which I left unspoken: I didn't know if I could handle the rejection of another birth parent.

"Liv, it's only the people who *don't* want you who act like Ali. Your father fought for you, didn't he? As a teenager, with limited resources, he tried to keep you. That doesn't say *I don't want you* to me."

He rested his chin on my head as I hugged his chest.

"I guess," I replied dubiously.

"Maybe he will be a screw-up. Maybe he won't be what you dreamed of or who you need, but at least he *wanted* you right? That's gotta count for something."

It counted for everything. Knowing that he wanted me was exactly why I was terrified to look for him. What if I found him and I wasn't what *he* wanted?

"You've changed, you know," Lucas murmured into my hair. "I know it sounds funny, when we haven't met that long ago, but I knew you then, and I see you now."

"Maybe not right now," I joked, staring around at the dark.

He laughed; it was such a lovely sound.

"But I know what you mean," I added.

Did he know how much he was a part of that change? I felt stronger with him, like I could be anyone, do anything—even just be myself. The thought of that didn't terrify me the way it used to. He saw me in a way that no one else had, and he hadn't run.

And another thought came, that perhaps I was thinking of my father not only out of selfishness, but because Lucas and I were together in this. He had just lost sight of his dad, and maybe by helping me find mine he could be encouraged to keep looking.

Yes, Lucas and I were the same. We didn't have to say things because we knew them. Just as he knew how much he meant to me, I knew how much I meant to him, and that he understood.

So we sat in silence for a while looking at the fireflies twinkling through the air above the water. Almost as an afterthought, Lucas said, "Who knows, maybe you'll be the one to save him."

His words shot straight into my heart. Save *him*? I had never considered that possibility. If my father was a screw-up, maybe it was only because I hadn't found him yet. If he was barely keeping it together, maybe that would all change when we were reunited. What if what he needed more than anything in the world was…me?

A slow smile began to spread across my face, and I could feel something welling up inside me. It was a feeling so fleeting and fragile that I hardly dared acknowledge it, for fear that it would disappear just as quickly as it came.

IT WAS HOPE.

BOOK 2 NOW AVAILABLE!

Order Your signed copy of Fractured today!

Order the e-book on Amazon here:

BOOK 3 NOW AVAILABLE!

Order Your signed copy of Reclaimed today!

Order the e-book on Amazon here:

PRE-ORDER BOOK 4 NOW!

Order Your signed copy of Redeemed today!

Order the e-book on Amazon here:

ACKNOWLEDGMENTS

Thank you Jesus for everything. Rob, thank you for being my real life love story. To my kids, thank you for letting me write uninterrupted and for being proud of me. You guys are my everything. Laura, thank you for accepting me as your sister no questions asked. James, thank you for wanting me & fighting for me. To my adoptive family, thank you for loving me as your own. H.V. & C.C. I hope things will be different someday. Cee, thank you for everything. To the three greatest teachers I ever had - LA Schmidt, Ms. Goodwin, and Cynthia Rowland, thank you for seeing something in me that I didn't yet see in myself. And finally, thank YOU dear reader for grabbing this book and supporting my author dreams.

xo Meggan

ABOUT THE AUTHOR

Meggan Larson is an award winning author (best selling on Amazon), course creator, wife, mom, and adoptee. She currently lives in Ottawa, Canada with her husband and three children. Through her indie publishing company, Starfish Stories Publishing, she helps the girl who reads all the books become the woman who writes and publishes them.

She lives her life around the concept of the starfish story, where a woman is tossing washed up starfish back into the ocean as they lay dying on the shore, and someone comes along and scoffs at her. He tells her she can't possibly make a difference because there are thousands and she'll never get to them all in time. She picks one up, tosses it back into the water, and says,

"It made a difference to that one."

Meggan wants to make a difference, even if it's just for one person.

Connect with her at hello@megganlarson.com or at her website at https://megganlarson.ca

Jump on her mailing list:

ALSO BY MEGGAN LARSON

Fractured: Book #2 in the Adopted series

Reclaimed: Book #3 in the Adopted series

Redeemed: Book #4 in the Adopted series

The Truth About Forgiveness (non fiction)

The Truth About Finding Joy in the Darkness (Anthology)

The Truth About Success (Anthology)

Being & Belonging (Anthology)

Starfish Stories, An Anthology Volume One

Excuse You? (A memoir)

Portraits (Anthology)

ABOUT STARFISH STORIES PUBLISHING

Starfish Stories Publishing: "Where the woman who reads all the books becomes the woman who writes them."

The Starfish Stories Publishing Company was founded in 2022. Its mission is to create a ripple effect of impact in the world through beautiful storytelling, authentic vulnerability, and inspiring messages of hope and belonging in a world desperate for real connection.

If you have a manuscript you would like us to consider, tap the QR code below and let's chat!

www.ingramcontent.com/pod-product-compliance
Lightning Source LLC
Chambersburg PA
CBHW020333310726
48979CB00015B/2353/J

* 9 7 8 1 9 9 0 4 1 9 6 7 6 *